Dragon

Book One of the Dragon Eye series

Chapter One

Prague, Czech Republic, September, 1993

Something's wrong.

Ozzie's growling—a deep, rumbling sound like she's summoning a vast army, their boots echoing as they march their way up from the depths of her throat. She's on the hall landing above the stairs, her doggy roar echoing down the steps toward the front door.

Our flat is one of those typical old Prague apartments. Most of the first floor is the butcher shop storefront. Our door is off to the left, tucked out of the way where it doesn't get much notice. Normally it's nice because people don't bother us. But under the circumstances, it's the worst possible set-up, because I can't see what's on the other side of the door without going down there and looking through the peep hole.

No way am I going down there, not with the way Ozzie's growling.

"What is it, Ozzie? What is it?" I whisper, as though talking at full volume might alert whatever's on the other side to our presence, and maybe set off whatever is about to happen, which I'm convinced will be bad.

Ozzie doesn't blink, doesn't turn my way or acknowledge me at all. She just lays her ears back flatter and growls more intently, as though impatient with the army that has not yet materialized, or the enemy that hasn't had the sense to flee.

I'd flee if I knew where to run.

See, Ozzie doesn't growl for anything. I've only ever heard her growl once before, when we were walking in a neighborhood of Prague that normally I didn't think was dodgy, but that day made me nervous for reasons I can't explain. Then Ozzie started this low growl, a commanding signal I couldn't ignore.

We cleared out of that neighborhood in a right hurry. I mean, we practically ran, which is saying something because Ozzie is a giant mixed breed mutt, mostly mastiff I guess, with equal parts Persian rug and trash compactor. She mostly eats and sleeps. She runs almost as rarely as she growls.

The next day I read in the paper there was a shooting in that neighborhood. Three people died and a bunch more got injured. We might have been among them if Ozzie hadn't known to growl.

I don't know how she knew. Dog instinct? Maybe she smelled something, a vaporous precursor of violence above the ubiquitous Czech scent of rye bread and brown gravy. All I know is, I trust her, and I take it bloody seriously when she growls.

So since she's growling right now for only the second time in the whole time I've known her, I know something has to be wrong. I feel called to action, to head out to battle, or flee, or something. The problem is, we're at home, in our flat above the butcher shop. We're not in a strange neighborhood. It's not like we can just run away or hurry home.

That terrifies me more than anything. I mean, where do you go when you're already in the safest place you know? I guess I do know of a safer place, the village where I grew up, but I haven't been there since I was a little girl, and I don't know where it is. If I knew, I'd be there now.

I'd be there in a heartbeat.

Instead I'm here, in Prague, working as a butcher and waiting for my father to come back for me, and right now I'm gripping the doorframe in fear of whatever's making Ozzie growl. I shuffle backward toward the kitchen, keeping one eye on Ozzie and one on the door. Once I'm just inside the kitchen doorway I reach for the phone and dial Ram's number by memory.

"Hello?" He answers on the first ring.

"Ozzie's growling."

"At what?"

"I don't know. At the front door? She's at the top of the steps."

"Stay out of sight. I'm coming over."

Ram doesn't say goodbye or anything. He's just gone. I got the impression he leapt out of his front door as he finished speaking. The word "over" seemed to barely make it through before the click that meant he'd hung up the phone.

I hang up, too, and crouch down low as though that might help. I can't see the front door anymore from this angle, but I can see Ozzie: her ears flat, her short hair on end, the low growl almost constant, never fading but never escalating to a bark.

I don't know what Ram's going to do, but I feel slightly better knowing he's doing *something*. He was Ozzie's owner before I came to Prague. He only lent her to me to keep me safe, and for company. I appreciate his gift on both counts. I'm also glad, because he seems to know that Ozzie's growling means danger — mortal danger.

Ram is this guy I work with. He lives across the street.

When my dad picked me up from school after I graduated this past spring, he brought me to Prague and hooked me up with the job at the butcher shop. My father introduced me to Ram and told me to trust him.

So I trust Ram. Also, he's pretty enormous. Not fat, I don't think, just really tall with these massive shoulders so that sometimes he has to turn a little sideways to fit through narrow doorways. It's hard to say how big he is, really, because his beard adds bulk and covers pretty much everything from just below his goggles to halfway down his coveralls.

Coveralls are like an insulated jumpsuit. We wear them in the back of the butcher shop because it's refrigerated, so even in the summer it's cold in there.

And the goggles are because of the blood splatter, in case you're wondering. The blood splatter from butchering. We both wear goggles, even though I don't splatter so much because, let's face it, I may be a pretty good butcher but I am nowhere near the slicing machine that is Ram.

In fact, the thought of Ram in his giant coveralls splattered in blood with his crazy long beard makes me feel slightly less frightened of whatever it is on the other side of the door that Ozzie is growling at.

If I was whatever is on the other side of the door, I would be scared of Ram.

Just as I'm starting to feel slightly less terrified, Ozzie stops growling. She perks her ears up and lumbers to her feet, heading down the stairs to the door, where she whines that little whine that means she wants to go out.

I'm still in the kitchen doorway, crouched halfway between hiding and standing, because Ram told me to stay out of sight and this is all I've got.

But Ozzie whines more insistently and lifts her paw like she's going to swipe at the doorframe, so I have to do something because if she actually *does* swipe at the doorframe and scratches the wood it's going to come out of my damage deposit. So I scramble down the stairs and open the door just a crack.

Ozzie pokes her head out.

"Get back inside." Ram is crouching on the stoop looking at what looks to me like nothing, but then it's pretty late in the evening and getting dark outside, so maybe there's something there and I just can't see it.

Fortunately Ozzie listens to Ram and pulls her head back in, so I close the door. I don't know what it was that was out there, but I know it was something, even if there's nothing there now.

Ozzie and I wait inside the doorway. I'm contemplating going back upstairs to stay out of sight, but Ram didn't necessarily say I had to anymore, and anyway, Ozzie isn't budging from by the door and I feel safest with her right beside me, so it's not like I'm going to leave her side, not voluntarily.

A minute or two later Ram raps on the door and I open it and he steps inside, sideways of course, in order to fit his shoulders through.

He doesn't look happy.

It's hard to say how I know this, because between the goggles and the beard, I can't properly see much of his face. His black hair is long and kind of shaggy, and hangs down to the lenses in the front. I guess he sort of has a moustache, but it's like one piece with his beard, so you can only see his mouth when he talks, and then just glinting white teeth.

So most of the time, all you can see is his nose, which isn't anything you'd ever notice if it wasn't the only part of his face you can see. It's a little hooked on the end, not like an eagle's beak or anything too dramatic, just a little manly sort of tip. It's neither large nor small, kind of medium-brown, either because he has a tan, or because he's of a darker-skinned, floppy-haired sort of race—I can't tell and I've never asked.

It's just a nose.

And right now, it's ever-so-slightly crinkled in a way that tells me Ram is not happy.

"They fled as I opened my door," he informs me in his ultra-deep voice that resonates from the vast recesses of his cavernous chest. "They're gone now."

"Who?"

Ram shakes his head. "You didn't see them?"

"I've been inside since we left work. Ozzie started growling. That's when I called you."

"Smell this, but stay out of sight." Ram opens the door and steps out just far enough for me to stick my head out and sniff. He stands in front of me so no one outside can see me.

We step back inside quickly.

"Did you smell it?"

I nod, trying to place the smell. It reminds me a little bit of the bugs that used to land on a halogen lamp in one of the classrooms at school. The heat from the lamp would fry them and they'd stink with an obnoxious, burning sort of stink.

It's like that stink, but without the burning, and fainter. And sort of evil…if evil has a smell.

The odor tugs at a memory I've tried to suppress, of the time when I was eight and my whole world changed.

A time of fear.

And hiding.

And darkness.

I push the memories away.

Ram gives me an intent look, which is pretty impressive when you consider I can't see his eyes due to his ever-present goggles. It's basically just the angle of his head and the way his nostrils flare ever-so-slightly. "If you smell that again, let me know immediately."

"What if you're not around?"

"Get to a safe place. Keep Ozzie with you at all times. Follow her lead."

Ram looks up the stairs. He seems to weigh something, as though he's trying to make a decision. Then he looks at me again, the same look that captures my attention and makes me think the danger he chased from my doorstep is still uncomfortably close. "I want you to pack a bag."

"Are we going somewhere?" A heady swirl of hope surges inside me — when my father left me in Prague, he said I'd stay here until he comes to get me and bring me home.

Home.

Leaving Prague means going home, the one thing I want more than anything.

"We may have to," Ram acknowledges with tangible reluctance. "For now, this is still the safest place for you. If we have to go, it may be on a moment's notice, and you won't have time to pack, or a chance to return. Put everything you care about and everything you need in a bag. Have it ready at hand so you can grab it and run if you have to."

My heart thumps with a beat that's more excited than afraid. "How will I know if I need to run?"

"I'll tell you. Don't attempt to go alone. Don't go anywhere alone. You'll go with me. I—" He pauses, looks around the beat-up old hallway with its flaking paint and lone light bulb. His voice drops a little, edged with an uncertainty I've never heard in his words. He's always so sure of himself, except for now. "This is still the safest place for you."

For a few seconds I study his face, but the light is dim and he is mostly goggles and beard. To be honest, I don't really know this man. I'm sure I wouldn't recognize him if I saw his face clean shaven. I don't even know how old he is. Older than me, surely, but not a whole lot older. He doesn't have any white hairs and he doesn't show any sign of going bald. Also, he's pretty spry. I'd be surprised if he was over thirty.

Not that it matters. All that matters is that my father told me to trust him, so I trust him.

With my life.

He turns toward the door. Pauses. "Are you going to be okay?"

I can't help thinking he's better equipped to answer that question than I am, but I muster up a smile that's supposed to be confident. "I'll be fine."

Ram slips sideways through the doorway. As he pulls the door closed after him, a wave of that strange smell from the stoop hits me with a whoosh, slapping to life the memories that were awakened when I sniffed outside the first time.

The terrified screams.

Running in darkness.

Hiding in caves and tunnels.

Hungry.

Scared, so scared.

And I realize the answer I just gave him was probably a lie, but he's gone now, and I'm not going outside to tell him I changed my mind.

Ozzie heads up the stairs toward bed beside me, but even her steps seem wary.

Chapter Two

My dreams are filled with the kind of stomach-churning anxiety that cut my childhood short at age eight, memories screaming like the winged creatures whose breath lit the night sky as I fled in terror.

Did I really see dragons that night?

I have feared them ever since.

Tonight they swoop through my nightmares, startling me awake too many times. I lie in bed panting, my thoughts swirling with theories.

Who am I?

What happened to my hometown?

All I know is, when our village was attacked, I spent three days in the caves with the other women and children from the village. Then my father came and took me away to Saint Evangeline's School for Girls on the Northumberland Coast of England, where it was foggy with dreary rain and I didn't know anyone, but worst of all, after going barefoot nearly all my life until then, I was forced to wear shoes.

Saint Evangeline's is supposed to be one of the safest schools on earth. That's their main selling point — safety. Sure, you get an education while you're there, but everyone attends because of their claims of safety. You can get an education at a prison, too, which is what Saint Evangeline's rather felt like.

Not that I've ever been to prison, but considering we had to wear uniforms and everything, and couldn't leave, and considering it's surrounded by high stone walls and armed security guards, I figure the only real difference between the school and a prison are the inmates.

The girls who go to Saint Evangeline's come from families who are willing to pay for safety — the Daughters of Privilege, I always called them, but never out loud. They're descended from royalty, actresses, CEOs of major corporations, pop singers, dictators, supermodels, and drug kingpins. Sometimes all in one family.

I've always wondered which group my father belongs to, but he's never let on. I never knew my real last name. When he enrolled me at Saint Evangeline's, my dad put me down under the last name *Smith*, which I'm pretty sure he picked because it's so generic. So that's no help.

I can only guess based on what I can remember, which isn't much. Dad made it a point to never refer to our town by name, only as "home" or "the village." All I know about my homeland is that it's sunny there, with mountains and a great sea, I think to the east.

And I know it's too dangerous for me to return.

It could be anywhere in the world. For a long time, based on my dark hair and brown skin, I thought perhaps Central America. Perhaps my father is a drug kingpin or dictator. But when I graduated and my father came to get me, he brought me as far as Prague and told me it wasn't safe to go any closer to home.

So perhaps my homeland is in the Balkans? I know Yugoslavia has been plagued by war. Bosnia, Croatia, and other regions whose names change with the pages of the calendar. Perhaps one of them is my home.

I don't know. But I won't find the answers inside my flat, and from what I understand, the danger is no longer content to keep me from my home, but is now seeking me out. It's no longer safe, not even here.

For once, not even my aching muscles or my dread of the cold stalls my steps as I dress for work and wash down a couple of runny eggs with black coffee.

Ozzie is reassuring (especially because she's not growling), but I just want to see Ram. He can be properly terrifying with all his butcher's swords strapped on, but he's on *my* side. That makes all the difference.

I arrive at work a few minutes before six, which is early for me. Ozzie sees me to the back door of the butcher shop and stands patiently watching until the heavy steel slab closes behind me. She'll stay there in the alley all day, moving only to switch from sunbeam to shade depending on the weather, lifting her head every time we toss out the big bones, which she crunches down to nothing with an efficiency that makes me oddly envious.

I step through the anteroom to the large refrigerated chamber where we work.

Ram is already inside, in full gear, fresh blood dripping from his coveralls and beard.

He's finishing a carcass as I walk in, and true to his usual habit, he doesn't pause to acknowledge I've entered, but remains focused on his work, his movements rapid but precise. With the sharp, slightly curved blade of the saber in his right hand he slices the last of the round steaks. Then he drops the sword back into the leather sling at his right hip, simultaneously pulling the cutlass from his left hip with his other hand. He swings the heavy-headed blade upward, and with a powerful blow, frees the steaks from the shank.

At the last second he grabs a pan with his right hand and catches the steaks as they fall, then turns to face me, depositing the pan on the stainless steel table, which is already heavy-laden with the rest of the butchered cow.

For a second he just stands there, dripping blood. Then he grabs a spray bottle from the table, aims it at his eyes, and douses his goggles, wiping them with a fresh towel.

It may be bloody in the butcher shop, but it's clean.

Well, sanitary at least.

I glance at the table of beef, mostly steaks with a few roasts and the inevitable kabob pieces. "Just one cow so far?"

"You're early."

"Not that early. What, did you pull a muscle? Need me to kick out a kink for you?" That's happened before. The man works like an ox for twelve, sometimes fourteen hours a day, usually with no ill effects, but every so often he gets something out of whack and needs me to shove it back in place. Last time it was his left shoulder, and I had to run at him and drive my elbow into the spot while he braced himself against the wall. It took three tries until it slammed back into place with a loud pop.

I can't imagine how that's healthy. It's just what happened.

But today he rolls his head slowly back-and-forth, sending out little neck-popping noises while the bloodied hairnet he wears on his beard dances a little jig.

The hairnet is for health code reasons. As near as I can tell it's almost useless, and I'm sure if we were inspected he'd have adequate warning to throw one on, but he still wears it every day, true to the rules, even if it makes him look silly.

As much as a man of his size can look silly.

"I went for a walk this morning, just to make sure." He glances toward the door.

I look behind me, too, as though there might be something there besides a steel slab and the door handle.

Nope, just a little blood splatter.

"Smell anything?" I ask.

I expect him to shrug off my question, to deny any danger, because that's the way he is—confident, nonchalant, bigger than any obstacle.

But he doesn't shrug or shake his head. He walks toward me, the volume of his voice turned down low, as though whatever was on my stoop last night might be out there right now, listening through the insulated walls of the refrigerated back room.

"I smelled it in Old Town, New Town, the Jewish Quarter, Castle District—"

"You crossed the river?"

"I've been all over town. I followed the smell."

"What does that mean, exactly?" I honestly don't even know what the smell is, just that it accompanies whatever Ozzie was growling at, so that must mean it's something fearsome. And it was there when the world of my childhood was torn apart. Oh, and it seems to even make Ram wary.

Fearsome, indeed.

Ram speaks in quiet tones, the hairnet on his beard bobbing like a bloody sock puppet. "I'd say it means they don't know where you are, just that you're in town somewhere. It's like they're looking for you."

I start to exhale, relieved.

"But if they were on your stoop last night—"

My breath catches in my throat, shoved back by the fear of whatever it is that makes that smell, that chased me from my home and forces me to live in exile still.

"But, who are *they*?" My heart pounds with theories. Are dragons real? Are they after me?

Ram only scowls, his mouth curving sourly in the midst of his beard. I don't think he's angry — I can't recall ever seeing Ram angry — but I brace myself anyway for whatever's going to come.

This is how we butt heads, Ram and I. No raised voices, no threats or violence. Just me asking for answers, and Ram refusing to provide them. We've been at this all summer, ever since school ended and my father brought me here.

Ram's silence doesn't surprise me. My father was always the same way. He visited me rarely enough while I was away in Britain in boarding school. I soon realized there was nothing to be gained by asking him questions — nothing but awkward silences, apologies, and longer gaps between visits.

The longer gaps may only have been coincidental, unavoidable delays on his part, but I felt them acutely, each day feeling more lost, abandoned, and unsure of myself and my place in this world.

So I'm not surprised that Ram denies me information. I'm used to it.

But now, instead of turning his back on me and starting in on another beef carcass, swords whipping through the air, singing the song of blade against bone, he meets my eyes.

As much as he can meet my eyes when his are covered. He's stepped closer to me, so close I could reach out and touch him, not that I have any desire to do so, bloody and hairy as he is. Close enough that his voice is little more than a rumble like distant thunder warning of a storm, his words clear only because I know the sound of his speech so well.

"They are the ones who attacked your village ten years ago. The ones who killed your mother. The reason you live in hiding still."

Pinprick stars flicker across my field of vision. Lightheaded, I reach for the table, but it's wet with the blood that oozes from the steaks, and my fingers slip.

Ram catches my elbow with one leather-gloved hand. His other arm keeps my sagging back from dropping to the floor. The prickling lights seem to mock me as they skitter away, chased from my sight by a surge of blood that pumps through my veins in a flood of embarrassment.

I'm a daft twit! How am I ever going to convince Ram to tell me *more* if I faint when he tells me anything?

Not that I actually fainted.

I just got a little lightheaded and couldn't quite stand upright. That's all.

Normally I'm a right steady person. Keep in mind, I dismember animals for a living. It takes a lot to make me woozy. But the mention of my mother's death, coupled with the reminder of the attack and my exile...it's too much, even for me.

And of course Ram knows I'm not a fainter, so now his mouth is clamped shut, a thin line barely visible amidst his beard.

"Who are they?"

Ram shakes his head. He's not going to tell me, not if it's going to bowl me over.

"I need to know. How can I avoid them if I don't even know what they look like?"

"The smell," Ram reminds me.

"What if my nose is stuffed up? What if the wind is blowing the wrong direction?" I lean hard on his arm as I struggle to put my full weight on my feet.

Ram doesn't look confident in my ability to stand on my own, but his arms move with me, propping me in a vertical stance.

I feel slightly less stupid from this angle.

Slightly.

"You've been training me to fight them?" I stare at the mirror-like surface of his goggles and wish I could see the answer there. Ram has been training me to fight— there was never any question about that. He's made it clear with his every instruction. The swordwork slices steaks, yes, hacks through cartilage and bone. We earn a living with our work, and Michal Jitrnicka, the butcher shop owner who works the front counter, is thrilled with our productivity and the lines that form to buy our precision-cut handiwork.

But every jab, every spear, every swing of the blades is a lesson, familiarizing me with the weight of my weapons, dulling the revulsion that would normally follow the stab of sword into flesh. Ram has been teaching me, not the clang of steel on steel, of fancy fencing like gentleman practice in sports clubs, wearing white uniforms and fighting like civilized men.

Ram has been teaching me to be a butcher.

To defend myself against my enemies with such effective swordwork my blade never touches theirs. To fell them before they ever have a chance to hurt me. To defend myself and my people from an attack such as the one that banished me from my homeland, should the enemy ever visit us again.

And they will visit us again.

I just don't know *where*, because until it is safe for me to return home, I am here.

There's a part of me that sort of hopes, twisted hope though it may be, that it's now too dangerous for me to stay here. Because if it's dangerous here—as dangerous as it is there—then there's no longer any reason for me to stay away.

Twisted, yes. But nonetheless, that's how I feel.

"Yes. They are the reason you must learn to fight." Ram releases me slowly, testing my ability to stand on my own before fully letting go.

"I need to know my enemy." I've stated these words before, but never with such conviction. "If they're at my doorstep, I need to know so I can defend myself. I can't afford to hesitate, but I'm so jumpy now I might attack anyone."

"Don't face them alone. That would be foolish and unnecessary. I will fight them for you. That's why I'm here."

"Then why are you teaching me to fight?" I stare at him through a long silence.

Just as I'm beginning to think he's not going to say another word, Ram answers with an unfamiliar strain in his voice. "If all else fails."

It takes me a moment to match his response to my question, to realize his words are the unexpected answer I'd asked for.

He swallows, the bobbing hairnet the only sign he's moved at all. "If *I* fail."

Chapter Three

Anger and fear fuel my work. I can't shake my dread—what if they come upon me suddenly?

Am I quick enough?

Strong enough?

I imagine the beef carcass in front of me as the enemy, and try to make each blow the one that defeats them.

We don't butcher like most butchers, with knives and saws, on tables, neat and methodical. We butcher with swords and daggers, standing upright as though facing an enemy. We start from the bottom of the carcass (that is, the neck—it's hung by a hook through the hind legs) and work our way up.

The heavy curved end of my cutlass frees the shank from the brisket, the arm roast from the chuck, and my saber makes quick work of the short ribs.

I set two pans on a low wheeled cart below the carcass, pull the daggers from their sheaths on my thighs, and slice crosshatches, carving out cubes of meat for stews or kabobs until I get to the ribs, the ones we turn into ribeyes, one of my favorite cuts of meat, second only to T-bones and, of course, porterhouse.

Okay, now I'm hungry.

Most days, I pull the long swords from their sheaths on the double baldrics that make an X across my back, and use the blades to cut ribeye steaks by first gently placing the edge of the blade in the precise spot where I'll need to make the cuts, making sure I've got the exact angle and proper alignment between the rib bones. Then I pull both arms back and bring the swords together swiftly, one on each side, cutting inward and downward toward the spine, slicing two steaks simultaneously, drawing the swords through and out toward me so that the two blades never touch. I then align my swords and make the next cut, and align them again before the next.

But today, I face the carcass like an opponent. I pull my swords out so swiftly the metal sings. I swing the blades wide, then bring them down and together, down and together, like a swimmer doing the butterfly stroke, like a butterfly fluttering its wings, except my wings are blades. This is how Ram always does it, how he's encouraged me to do it, but I've always been too careful before. I wanted my steaks to be pretty.

Not today.

If the enemy is after me (whoever they are, the ones who killed my mother and chased me from my homeland) I need to be quick far more than I need to be pretty.

I slam the razor-sharp metal through the meat, slice after slice, working my way past the ribeyes to the T-bones, the porterhouse, the sirloins, pausing only to free the flank steak with my saber.

When there's nothing left but the hind legs I stand back, panting from the effort, to evaluate the meat piled in the pans below.

Ram has stopped working and is watching me. He is grinning.

This is most unusual, and, dare I say it? — a little unsettling. He has very white, straight teeth, and his smile (at least as much as I can see of it through his beard) is handsome.

Weird. I really didn't expect that. Ram is a giant looming force, singing blades and cloaking hair. On some level, I've always assumed he's hair all the way down, that if you shaved him you'd end up with just a pile of hair, swords, and shoes.

Not this grin that's watching me as though I've done something dazzling.

Probably I am only imagining the handsomeness. I mean, he did rather save me from whatever Ozzie was growling at last evening, so perhaps my perception of him has gone fuzzy. I must remember, this is the man who makes me work like a slave twelve hours each day, who refuses to help me get home, who won't even tell me where home is, though I know he knows.

I glower at him. "What?"

He is supposed to take the hint and stop grinning, but instead he steps toward me, his smile still broad. "You're doing it. You've got it." Crouching, he plucks a couple of steaks from the pans and holds them toward me, flat on his palms. "Very good. Even thickness. You're still cutting at a bit of an angle, though. See how these are parallelograms?" He tips his hands to exaggerate the flaw.

"They're still even thickness. They'll cook fine."

"But you've got to get the *movement* right."

"Why?" I'm out of breath, panting even, from the exertion of cutting so many steaks so swiftly. Maybe I make it look easy, but it *is* hard work, just the same.

"It's important. Besides, if you do it wrong, you'll get a cramp in your shoulders. Here." He shoves the dangling hindquarters aside and grabs the next carcass in the queue, scooting it along the hook track above, positioning it above the waiting pans.

"I wasn't done with that." I point feebly at the hindquarters.

"I want you to get this right. You're so close." He swings his cutlass, with one mighty blow lopping the shank and brisket free from the rest of the cow. After returning his sword to its holster, he plants me in front of him and guides my arms in a swooping motion, so similar to what I was doing moments before, but with a flatter angle and more of a twist at the end. "See there? Feel that? Good form reduces your odds of getting injured and cuts better steaks. It also helps ensure your blows are accurate."

"Okay. Stand back." I can feel the difference in the swing. As Ram steps back, I step toward the carcass and bring the blades together just as he showed me. Two steaks fall atop the mountains of meat. Two more. Two more.

Still tired from my marathon effort with the last animal, I pause, replace my swords in their scabbards and pick up two steaks, holding them out to Ram for his inspection.

What is it with this guy? He's still grinning. Seriously, Ram never grins and Ozzie never growls, not until the last ten hours or so. At least Ram's smile isn't quite so big right now, but I still study his face to prove to myself he is not actually handsome, that it was just a trick of the light or my overwhelming shock at seeing him smile in the first place.

Hairy and goggley, yes, but also sort of good looking. Weird.

"Much better. I think you've got that down." He hoists the heaping pans of steak from the floor cart and carries it to the table. I grab the nearest wheeled rack and help him load the pans.

The cut meat goes to the next room, where Michal's teenage daughters, Zusa and Tyna, wrap what needs to be wrapped, further process anything that needs further processing (like the ground beef and sausages) and arrange it attractively in the windows, all while smiling and giggling and flirting with the young men among the customers who come to the shop.

In a logical sense, Zusa and Tyna are probably a lot like me. I mean, I'm eighteen and they're both right around there, sixteen and nineteen, I think. But I feel like we have little in common, and I'm not just talking about the language barrier. I may not know much Czech, but they know a bit of English, and all three of us have conversational German, enough to chat together — which we've done for a few moments now and then, mostly when I first came here.

Not that I can blame them for not befriending me. I'm probably a little freakish, with my swords and blood-stained coveralls. And I admit I don't linger too long in the doorway when I shove the meat cart their way. "Děkuji, Tyna. Děkuji, Zusa." I let go of the cart and wave.

"Děkuji, Ilsa!" They wave back, friendly enough, but that's the end of it. Tyna grabs the cart, turns her back to me and navigates the narrow walkway of the front room.

The door closes.

And that's the end of my normal peer interaction. To be honest, I didn't fare much better at Saint Evangeline's, even without the swords and bloodstained coveralls. I went to school with real princesses, with girls whose families had so much money they could buy themselves a country, if they wanted (or so girls claimed whenever someone of noble birth tried to pull rank).

Since I didn't even know where I was from, I was at a disadvantage from the start. Somewhere along the way, I stopped trying to gain acceptance. The last time I can really recall having friends was in the village.

Homesickness wells up inside me again, and I turn to face the carcass I still need to finish.

My enemy.

The ones who stole my childhood and killed my mother.

My blades sing again as I pull them from their sheaths. This time, I get everything right—the angle, the force, the speed, the cut. Steaks fall in piles in the pans below. This time I finish everything, right up to the hind shank and hock.

When I finish this time, I'm panting. I grab a spray bottle and clean the lenses of my goggles while they're still on my face, mopping up sweat along with blood.

I glance at Ram and he's looking my way.

Grinning, again.

What's up with that?

*

By noon I'm starving.

Ram must have guessed I'd be hungry after all that work, because I see him carry five large porterhouse steaks through the back door as I'm finishing the hindquarters.

This is the best part of my job, the best perk in the history of job perks. We get to eat all we can of whatever meat we want.

My first day working here, I was a little weirded out by the hanging carcasses and the swords (I think swords are smashing, and all, it was just a big adjustment getting used to their sharpness and using them on flesh and all that). In fact, by lunchtime that first day, I was starting to think my father had brought me here to punish me, which was sort of devastating on top of my crushed hope that I might finally get to go home.

Then Ram went outside with the steaks, and minutes later called me to join him in the anteroom. There's a table in there and a couple of big plates — platters, really. No silverware. No steak knives or anything remotely civilized like that.

Ram pushed a platter of seared steak my way and grunted something vague that might have been, "Here," but also could have been a belch. Then he picked up one of the steaks on his platter and tore into it with his teeth.

Okay, big confession: I like meat.

This was a huge no-no at school, where something like two-thirds of the girls were vegetarians, and even those who ate meat only did so in tiny amounts. I used to offer to clear the tables on the nights when we had chicken, and I'd eat the bones all the way back to the kitchen, with my body turned sideways so no one could see. Fortunately most of the girls were in a habit of ignoring me, so I rarely got caught.

And when I did get caught, I denied it. "Who eats chicken bones?" I'd scoff. "That's disgusting." They never pushed the issue — I think they were scared of what they saw, so I got away with it.

Deep down, though, I knew the truth. I am a disgusting person. Normal people don't eat chicken bones, no matter how delicious and crunchy and irresistible they are, and no matter how long it's been since they got a good meal with real meat in it.

So, seeing Ram pick up the steak and tear into it with his teeth made me stare, gobsmacked, unsure how to proceed. For the past ten years I'd had to exercise strict self-control around meat, going to elaborate lengths to scarf down scraps in secret. And here was this hairy mountain of a man, openly eating a beautiful steak with no compunction and no silverware.

Then—I can still picture this vividly—Ram sort of sucked in a long strip of fat and flesh he'd torn from the steak with his teeth, and with the food still dangling against his beard, he asked, "What's the problem?"

I'm sure my mouth was hanging open.

In fact, I was probably drooling. I stammered something about utensils, and he told me there weren't any, and gestured to the steak and told me to eat.

And I did. I picked up the porterhouse and tore into it and loved it.

Lunch has been my favorite time of day ever since, with the possible exception of supper, which is my other favorite time. Ram flash-grills the meat—I don't know how he does it, exactly, but he sears the outside crispy while the inside is bloody and cool.

It is the best food ever, made even better by the fact that I can eat it openly, without restraint or embarrassment, even sucking the marrow out of the bones.

So today, Ram grills five steaks—three for him and two for me. And that was just lunch.

We ate the same again for supper, and then Ram made cookies for dessert. Meat cookies—which are basically hamburgers, sometimes with chunks of onion or mushroom and seasonings inside. Meat cookies are my favorite kind of cookies.

In all, it's a great day at work, other than the part where Ram smiled at me, which was unnerving. I mastered the butterfly maneuver and cut up more meat than ever before.

Satisfied, once I'm finished helping Ram clean up for the day, I step through the door to the anteroom and freeze.

I can hear scratching and whining coming from the other side of the exterior door. Immediately I realize Ozzie is on the other side. She wants in.

"Ozzie, what's wrong?" I ask as I cross the room and open the door just wide enough to get a decent look at Ozzie.

Then I scream.

Chapter Four

The smell is strong, far stronger than the night before, and Ozzie's muzzle is a bloodied mess. I'm torn between holding the door open so she can come in, and slamming it shut to keep the evil out.

Fortunately I don't have to make the choice myself. Ram runs up behind me, scoops up Ozzie like an infant, and whisks her inside.

I slam the door closed and lean my back against it.

"There's a drop bar, there." Ram gestures with his head, his arms full of the wounded dog. I look up behind me and see the heavy beam, which I drop securely into place behind the iron catch plate.

"Back inside," Ram says, turning to the door that leads back into the refrigerated area.

We've never let Ozzie inside before. In fact, I'm pretty sure the health code is strictly against animals in the prep room, not even wearing hairnets. But under the circumstances, I don't care about the rules. I push the insulated door open and hold it wide so Ram can carry Ozzie through.

He lays her on the stainless steel table we'd scrubbed down minutes before. I run to the corner where we keep the first aid kit.

By the time I turn around again, Ram has sprayed Ozzie's bloodied face with the cleanser we use, which is mostly water with a mild antibacterial antiseptic—food grade, of course. It probably won't feel the greatest if it gets in her eyes, but that's the least of our worries at the moment, and anyway, Ozzie has the sense to pinch her eyes shut the moment Ram points the bottle her way.

Ram dabs gently at Ozzie's face with a clean cloth. I circle around the table, making soothing sounds and checking her over for other injuries. She doesn't appear to have any others, which is a relief.

"How bad is it?" I come to a stop next to Ram and inspect the damage myself. This time, I grab the table with both hands and breathe in slowly, purposefully. I promise you, I don't usually go woozy at the sight of blood. I live amidst blood, splattered with blood.

But this blood is different, because it's coming out of Ozzie. And I love Ozzie. Three days after my dad left me in Prague, before Ram had technically lent me his dog, I spent half an hour one day hugging Ozzie and crying into her fur. Crying because I had *so* hoped my father would bring me home, but he hadn't. Crying because I work in a refrigerator with dead animal carcasses and a hairy guy whose eyes I can't even see.

That day, Ram found me crying with Ozzie and told me I could take the dog home with me.

Best. Gift. Ever.

And now I'm sniffling again, because Ozzie is the only creature on earth who lets me cry on her shoulder and now she's hurt and bleeding and probably got injured trying to protect *me* from the nameless faceless enemies who've destroyed my life, who Ram will tell me nothing about.

And as I'm standing here, gripping the cold stainless steel table and watching Ram dab at the slash marks across Ozzie's face, I realize a couple of things.

One: I am sick of not knowing my enemy.

And two: I am tired of waiting, doing nothing while Whoever-They-Are circle around us, moving in closer, preparing to attack us, hurting the dog I love.

"We've got to go," I blurt in a helpless, choked voice.

Ram doesn't look up from his dabbing. "I'm going to take care of these cuts first, and then check out the alley before I carry her back to your flat. Just be patient."

"No. I mean, we've got to get out of town. It's not safe here anymore."

"Where are you going to go? Back to Saint Evangeline's?"

"No. Home."

"You can't go home yet. Your father will come for you when it's safe." Ram finishes dabbing and gets out some ointment and bandages.

"I don't care if it's not safe there. It's not safe here, either."

"You can't go home until your father comes. You need someone to go with you, to protect you and show you the way."

"Why can't *you* do that?" This solution seems glaringly obvious to me. I don't understand why Ram doesn't see it.

"My job is to teach you how to fight, and to keep you safe *here*."

"Fine. Just tell me how to get home. I know how to fight. I can defend myself."

Ram is scowling, either at the cuts on Ozzie's face — which fortunately don't look too deep — or at my suggestion.

Which, I will admit, is probably not the most prudent plan I've ever come up with, but at least it's a plan. Ram just wants to hang around until the enemy shows up. And as Ozzie's injuries prove, that's a barmy plan.

"You will wait for your father," Ram concludes. "Be patient and calm down."

I try to be calm. I think Ram is implying that it's upsetting to Ozzie the way I'm getting worked up, but you know what? It's upsetting to me that Ozzie got hurt and Ram won't even acknowledge the danger is real enough for us to do something. "Can you at least call my dad? Talk to him? Tell him we're getting attacked here, and we need him to come?"

"That would give away our location."

I gesture to the gashes on Ozzie's nose. "They don't already know where we are?"

Ram shakes his head. "This is just a guess. If they knew, it would be worse."

Ozzie whimpers as Ram tries to wrap gauze over her wounds. "You're upsetting her. Why don't you go wait at the front of the store? Keep Tyna and Zusa company."

"Fine." I'm tired of arguing with Ram, anyway, so I stomp through the door to the storefront.

Except Zusa and Tyna aren't there. Neither is Michal. The lights are still on, though. The only person around is a guy wearing a gray shiny blazer over a black t-shirt with jeans, a classic tall-dark-and-handsome guy, standing at the meat counter, waiting to be helped.

I'm so taken aback at seeing him there instead of the others, I blurt out, "Can I help you?" half a second before I remember this is Prague, and most people don't speak English.

But he smiles and says, "I'd like to look at your meat."

Now I know why Tyna and Zusa are always flirting with the customers. I'd never thought about it before, but when a guy asks to see your meat, and he says it while smiling like that, and he's looking at you over the counter like *that*, it sounds really flirtatious.

Or maybe I just think it does because I have zero experience with guys. Obviously there weren't any at Saint Evangeline's, and Ram doesn't count.

This guy, however? Yeah, this guy counts. I try not to blush (and fail). "What cut would you like to see?" I reach for the sliding door behind the meat counter, in the section where we keep the T-bones and porterhouse—the nicest steaks. He looks like the kind of guy who likes the nicest steaks.

"What is the best thing you have?"

I lift out a big porterhouse and extend it toward him, in the back of my mind wondering where the Jitrnickas went, and why they left the store unlocked with the lights on, and if they're coming back. But mostly I'm thinking about the fact that I'm holding a conversation with a real live guy. A cute one, even. Okay, so probably he's older than I am, but not too old. Twenties or so. And he has a cleft in his chin.

"What do you think of this?" I hold the steak out for him to see.

He leans against the glass front of the counter, close enough I can feel his warm breath on my arm (I've been hanging out in a refrigerator all day, so a little warmth makes a big difference).

"This steak is sword-cut." He sounds impressed.

"How can you tell?"

"Knives pull the grain of the meet as they pass through the fibers. Swords move more swiftly. They preserve the cell structure so the meat retains more of its natural moisture and flavor. It's a far superior cut, but a technique few practice anymore." His English is perfect, as is his smile. He is tall but slender, his hair dark, though his skin is fairer than mine. I can't tell his ethnicity, though his nose and chin are somewhat pointy, his cheekbones high, his eyes hidden by sunglasses. "You must charge a premium for such a fine product."

"Uh, yeah." I look around for a price sheet, madly wishing one of the Jitrnickas would show up and save me from my own ignorance. The Czech koruna was only recently converted from the Czechoslovak koruna, and I'm not really familiar with either of the denominations because I've only been in Prague a few months and I spend most of my time in the refrigerator or sleeping. "I think there's a sign, maybe? Can you see it from that side?"

The guy crouches down and peers into the meat case through the glass. I do the same from this side, looking fruitlessly for a price label somewhere. When I glance up to see if he's getting impatient, I find him looking at me.

Studying me.

I'm not even kidding. His eyes are locked on my face and he doesn't even do that self-conscious look-away-I-wasn't-really-looking thing like most people do in airports and bus stations when you catch them staring off into space in your direction.

And then he smiles. It's a jolly fine smile, but I get the impression he knows it's a fine smile. He knows he's gorgeous and he's using that to his advantage!

Okay, I may be naïve about guys but no way am I letting this bloke sweet-talk me into selling him a porterhouse for a reduced rate.

If only I knew how much the steak is supposed to cost.

"Let me just go in back and ask—"

"Actually, please." He reaches across the counter and touches my hand.

The hand holding the steak.

It's like we're holding hands, and also holding a porterhouse between us. This would be romantic if I knew the bloke.

"My name is Ion."

And now I know him.

"I'm Ilsa." My name is no sooner out of my mouth than I wonder if I'm supposed to be sharing that information around, especially with my father's arch-enemies on the loose, looking for me, and I don't even know what they look like.

Well, blimey, if I'm not supposed to tell people my name, maybe Ram should have said so. He kind of sucks at protecting me, you know? Speaking of, where is he? And where are the Jitrnickas? It's pretty much dark outside by now and I don't know why the butcher shop would still be open this late, and did I mention Ion has a nice smile?

He also has kind of longish hair, probably shoulder length. It's dark and full and slightly wavy, swept back from his face in a cosmopolitan look that pairs smartly with the shiny gray of his blazer.

"Ilsa." Ion repeats my name, beaming a smile that seems to say he's glad to meet me, maybe even glad to have found me, although that seems weird.

The door behind me opens and Ram walks through, talking. "We can go —"

He stops talking.

I hasten to make introductions as Ion pulls his hand quickly away from mine. "This is —"

"Ion." Ram says the name just as I say it.

"Hello, Ram." Ion is no longer smiling.

"Do you two know each other already?" My question seems appropriate, but neither of them bother to answer it. They're glaring at each other like a couple of stag deer ready to lock horns, like in one of the nature shows they were always making us watch at Saint Evangeline's, on account of we could only watch educational stuff.

While wearing shoes.

Yeah, I still resent that last part.

The guys are silently staring each other down so I put the porterhouse away and close the meat case. I get the feeling Ion's visit was never about the steak.

"How did you get in here?" Ram's nostrils flare with something seething. Anger? Threat?

"The shop was open." Ion's smile is back, but it feels fake.

I'm starting to worry about the Jitrnickas now, especially considering that Ozzie was attacked, so I clarify, "Unattended?"

Ion shrugs off my question without answering, which does *not* make me like or respect him, in case you were wondering. He's talking to Ram like I'm not there. "Elmir sent me to find you."

Elmir is my dad. Ion knows my dad? My dad sent him?

I miss my dad. I miss my home.

"He says you need to bring Ilsa home now."

You know what? I think I was wrong about Ion. He's a great guy. I kind of want to hug him.

But Ram, who seems to jolly well want to be kicked in the shins, just glares at Ion. "Elmir gave me specific instructions."

"To wait here until he comes?" Ion nods, a slow nod that leaves his head dipped an extra-long second, almost like he's bowing. "His orders have changed. He sent this, as proof his request is sincere." He whips a card from his pocket and holds it out toward Ram.

Ram swallows visibly, which is quite a feat considering his enormous beard, but then I'm standing off to his side, so I can see his neck muscles working.

"What is it?" I take a step closer, trying to see what it says on the card.

Ram takes the card from Ion and passes it to me.

"It's a picture of your mother."

Chapter Five

I have never seen a picture of my mother before this moment. She died before I was born (I know, I know — the girls at school had a heyday with that one, too, but I was always told she died *before* I was born, so I believe it, even if it's not medically feasible) and my dad could never bring himself to speak of her, because he loved her so much and misses her.

For a flickering second, as Ram hands me the card, I wonder how I'm supposed to know if the picture is really of my mother, if Ion's sign is actually proof my father sent him, when I don't know what my mother looks like. It could be a picture of anybody.

Then I look at the picture, and I know.

It's me.

No, not me. I have my father's coloring — his jet black hair, rusty brown skin, and his eyes, which are a weird shade of brown that, to be honest, almost look red.

The eyes never helped with my popularity issues at Saint Evangeline's.

But other than her coloring, which is obviously fair in spite of the fact that the picture is old and sepia-toned, the woman looks like me. She has my full lips, bent in a sweet smile. The cheeks that are a little rounder than I'd like. The eyes, big and expressive under high arched brows, which give away every secret and lose at poker, like whenever I was invited to play the covert night games, which I'm sure only happened because the girls knew it would be easy to win my money.

Something great and tragic wells up in my throat. My mother was beautiful. Never mind that she looks like me. In her own way, she was beautiful. I hold on to the card, being careful not to bend the picture. It is *such* a gift.

"Now is not a good time," Ram informs Ion. "The yagi are swarming. They attacked my dog this evening."

So, our enemies are called *yagi*, hmm? It's amazing what I've learned since Ion showed up. I like this guy more and more. Why couldn't Ram have told me that much already? At the same time, the word sounds familiar. *Yagi.* Doesn't that mean *enemy*?

But I can't think about how I know the word. Ion is talking.

"They are precisely the reason you must come now. They are hunting for Ilsa. While they search for her here, we can sneak away. There are fewer on the path home."

Home. The word echoes in my ears. I turn to Ram. "He's right. We should go now."

Ram doesn't look happy at all. I know he likes being in charge, and he is really, really, really serious about following my dad's instructions. To. The. Letter.

I'm pretty sure my dad is his boss, the only one who can tell him what to do. Ram isn't fond of being questioned, let alone opposed, and certainly not outnumbered. "Come in back. We'll discuss it."

Ram locks up the storefront and turns off the lights while I lead Ion through the back to the anteroom where Ozzie is waiting, resting in a heap near the back door as if to block the entrance from outsiders. I run over to see how she's doing, and she thumps her tail weakly in greeting.

To my relief, it looks like Ram did a fine job wrapping her injuries without blocking her nose or eyes. I place a hand on her back and pat her gently, while Ion turns to face Ram as he enters.

Ram fires off protests. "How would you have us travel? The dog is injured. She cannot make the trek on foot. Nor can we bring her or our weapons on trains and planes."

"I have a car."

Ion is my hero.

Ram looks as though he's trying to think of another excuse, a reason not to go along with Ion's proposal, but he can't, and this makes him even more frustrated. "At the very least, we should wait until morning."

"Night is the best time to leave—under the cover of darkness." Ion's reasoning makes plenty of sense to me, never mind that I'm exhausted from a day of butchering that was even more rigorous than usual.

"Ilsa and I are tired," Ram points out.

"You can sleep in the car while I drive."

Ram turns to me. "Did you pack a bag?"

"It's just inside my door. I can grab it on a moment's notice."

I can tell Ram is running out of objections. What I don't understand is why he feels so strongly the need to object. If my dad says it's time for me to come home, it's time. It's past time. I want to be there now. Yesterday. Ten years ago and every day since.

Ram makes one more futile protest. "We'll need to bring our weapons. They'll cause trouble at the border crossings."

Ion only laughs. "I've gotten far worse than a few swords and daggers across the borders, in more desperate times than these. Let's get your bags and go."

I study the picture of my mother and wonder vaguely in the back of my mind what Ion could possibly do for a living to have crossed borders with weapons so many times. He doesn't look *that* much older than I am.

Ram makes every aspect of their discussion sound like an objection, but finally, he and Ion agree on the next several steps. Ram is going to round up our weapons—swords, daggers, and their sheaths, and hand them off to Ion. Then Ram will carry Ozzie and meet Ion in front of the building.

Between the two of them, the men will not leave me unattended, not even for a moment. Ram is adamant about this. I consider pointing out to him that I'm not completely helpless, but the red stain of blood has already begun to seep up through the gauze of Ozzie's bandages, reminding me how real the danger is.

Ram and I select our favorite swords, and Ion takes the selected weapons. While Ram scoops up Ozzie, I rush to the back door and hold it open for him. The evening air is slightly humid. The scent of yagi hangs heavy in the alley, and for an instant I'm tempted to slam the door shut again.

But no, we have to go. We must pass through the scent of evil if I'm ever going to get home.

Ram makes a face, but he carries Ozzie outside ahead of me, looking about warily as I come up behind him and close the door.

"Should we leave a note for the Jitrnickas?" It occurs to me that we don't even know for sure if they're okay. I mean, if Ozzie was attacked, who knows what might have happened to them? Not that they ever check out with us before leaving for the evening, but they're usually still closing up the front of the shop after we've cleaned up the back and left for the night.

"They've always known we would leave suddenly. If anything, they're surprised we've stayed this long. They will be safer once we're gone." As Ram talks we trek down the alley toward the street. I look up, above my little flat, to the third floor apartment that straddles the two storefronts, Michal's butcher shop and the mending business his wife operates next door, which she shares with her sister, who lives in the second floor flat next to mine.

As I'm looking up, Tyna opens a window, mutters something in Czech about the smell outside, and closes the window again, but not before I hear easy laughter in the room behind her.

The Jitrnickas are fine. The yagi have not bothered them.

This is a huge relief to me, even if Ram already predicted it.

Ion puts our swords in the front storage boot of his four-door Skoda (which have the engine in the rear) and Ram gently settles Ozzie into the back seat.

I'm standing dumbly on the curb, watching to make sure Ozzie doesn't whimper too much, when Ion says to me, "Let's grab your bag."

I dart up the stairs with Ion behind me. My bag is where I left it, next to the kitchen door. It's pretty big for a backpack, but still, it looks small when you consider that everything I need is packed inside, including a spare toothbrush. I don't have much. The pans and dishes in the kitchen belonged to the Jitrnickas. I won't need my coveralls on the road. There isn't much else. Jeans, t-shirts, a jacket in case it gets cold.

But I'm used to the cold.

"Got everything?" Ion asks. He looks calm, but eager to get going.

"Yup." I'm eager, too.

Ram steps out from the front door of his flat across the street as Ion and I head for the car. Ram pauses at the curb, though no cars are coming and it's safe to cross. He sniffs the air and his brow furrows as he turns to look down the street.

I look, too.

Nothing appears out of the ordinary. Swirls of graffiti mar the once-lovely facades of Baroque buildings, but that is not unusual for this neighborhood. It's long past sunset and the buildings are heavily shadowed.

The shadows bother me. They could hide anyone, or anything.

Ram darts across the street toward me. His hand at my back guides me into the rear seat. Ozzie takes up much of the seat, but I place her head on my lap and we both fit.

"Let's get going," Ram tells Ion as the pair close their doors and Ion starts the car.

I'm stroking Ozzie's back, but I look up as we pull away from the curb. The shadows shift behind me, and shapes like men step out into the fringes of the light. Two, three...a dozen.

Men? Or yagi? I open my mouth to say something to Ion and Ram, but we turn the corner, and whatever I saw passes out of sight.

I clamp my mouth closed. We're leaving them behind, so there's no point saying anything that might make Ram or Ion decide to stick around for even a moment longer.

As far as I'm concerned, we can't get away fast enough.

"Which way are we headed?" I ask as Ion navigates through Prague's narrow streets.

"East." Ram's tone is final, communicating that he knows I'm going to ask for more specifics, but he's going to refuse to give them. I know that tone well from previous conversations. So many other times, I've given up asking when he used that tone.

But Ion wasn't with us those other times.

I keep asking. "How far east?"

As I'd hoped, Ion is not so close-lipped. "We'll go through Krakow—"

"Budapest," Ram counters.

"Poland, then Ukraine," Ion insists, turning a corner sharply as though to take us there this very second.

"Slovakia, Hungary, Romania, Bulgaria." Ram's deep voice bellows the name of each country like commands, listing places that mark a far different route than the one Ion suggested. "We'll go south, through Istanbul."

"North through Russia." Ion talks right over the top of Ram, as though he's not even afraid of him, which is craziness. They may be close in height, but Ram is huge compared to Ion. Although, to be honest, I don't know how much of that is beard.

"Russia is too dangerous."

"South is too dangerous."

"We'll be east of the Balkans, east of trouble," Ram insists. "Russia is too dangerous."

"It's only civil unrest."

"It's not the civilians I'm worried about."

The two bicker like that, weighing the pros and cons of countries I only know about from geography class and news broadcasts—usually bad news—and I stroke Ozzie's fur and wonder where it is we're ultimately going. Where is my homeland? Who am I?

"Where is it we're ultimately going?" I ask in a lull, while Ion studies a street sign and Ram basks in the wake of an undisputed assertion.

Ion makes up his mind and turns left. "To your home. To your father."

"But where is that?"

"Ah—" Ion begins.

"She doesn't need to know yet." Ram cuts him off.

"We're going there, Ram," I remind him. "You can tell me now. We're going there, no matter what."

Ion laughs. I'm not sure what the laugh means and I don't know if I like it. Is he laughing because I've made my point? Or because I don't know where I'm from? Is he laughing at Ram or me?

Ram's voice rumbles through Ion's laughter. "Azerbaijan." He states flatly. "Your home is in the mountains of Azerbaijan."

I sit quietly in the back seat, unable to respond. The word is a foreign one. It's one of those countries formed when the USSR fell apart. I think. I'm really not sure. Nor do I know where it is. Somewhere along one of the edges of Russia, most likely. Somewhere past Poland and Bulgaria.

The tension leaves my body as I settle back into my seat, and Ozzie sniffs a little sigh.

We're going home. And Ram has finally, *finally* relented to tell me where home is.

It's just that now, I feel as lost as ever. Because home is suddenly a long word I can't spell, and know nothing about. And I wonder if maybe I've been gone too long, if the home I've dreamed of is too strange a place now. If I'll be a stranger there, too.

Ion drives slowly down a dark road. I watch the shadows shift outside. I'm not sure if it's the moonlight playing through the clouds, or if those are more men, or yagi, or just my fear playing tricks on my eyes.

But I can't help wondering if maybe Ram was right. Maybe we should have stayed in Prague. Maybe home was just a dream, anyway, and the road is too dangerous to travel.

Chapter Six

We leave Prague behind. The countryside is dark. When I peer out my window, all I can see are shadows and the reflection of my own face, the only Azerbaijani face I know.

Except that I'm half Scottish — on my mother's side. She attended Saint Evangeline's when she was young, although I scoured the old yearbooks for anyone resembling me and never found her. Now I look again at the picture in my hand.

No, I never saw this picture, or this face among the others.

Questions rise in my throat, but I don't know how to put them into words, and I doubt Ram or Ion would answer me anyway. They're too busy arguing about going north or south. And it's not for lack of asking that I don't know my mother's name.

And anyway, I guess I do know other Azerbaijanis. My father, and presumably Ram and Ion, and of course, everyone I knew before I left, though I can't recall much anymore. I had a friend, Arika, who lived two doors down from me. She had a doll with a beautiful embroidered cloth face. I don't remember the doll's name, but I can picture it.

I can picture the doll more clearly than the face of my friend.

The questions knot in my throat. I glance around the back seat and spot a road atlas on the floor.

Eastern Europe and the Caucasus.

Carefully, trying not to disturb Ozzie, who's snoring on my lap and who needs her sleep, I reach for the atlas, snag the tip of one corner between my fingers, pull it closer, and lift it above the dog.

Eastern Europe is basically everything between the Czech Republic and Russia, including parts of Russia, depending on who you ask. But I'm not familiar with the Caucasus. I flip to the Index, then the introduction, then I know.

The Caucasus is my home. The mountain countries between the Black Sea and the Caspian Sea—Armenia, Georgia, and Azerbaijan—they're the Caucasus. The people there are Caucasians.

I laugh aloud.

"What?" Ram stops arguing with Ion and turns to me.

"I'm Caucasian." I hold the atlas so he can see. "I always checked the box for 'other/unknown/mixed.' Turns out, I was probably the only real Caucasian at Saint Evangeline's."

Ram shoots me a wry smile. "Semantics."

"I know." Given how much the other girls liked to hold their every perceived advantage over my head, the truth strikes me as particularly ironic, and kind of funny. "I never understood why we had to check a box at all. There should only be one box. Human. We're all human."

Ram opens his mouth as though to say something, maybe even argue with me, but Ion makes a snorting noise and Ram turns back to the front of the car so I can no longer see any of his face, just thick black hair and silence.

I don't know what that's all about. We're human, obviously. I return my attention to the atlas, to the section on Azerbaijan. It contains a couple of paragraphs about the country, which are fortunately in English. I don't think any of the countries in the atlas actually speak English, but it's one of the most common secondary languages people study, and perhaps the only one the mapmakers figured their target audience might share.

I read the introduction.

Historically known as the 'Land of Fire' due to jets of natural gas that burn as they escape from the ground, and the practice of fire worship, Azerbaijan is reawakening as it emerges from Soviet Control. Its rich culture is largely unknown to those who live beyond its borders. Many regions are accessible only on horseback or with a four-wheel-drive vehicle, so the close-knit communities of the remote areas remain a mystery to outsiders.

From its snow-capped mountains to its fertile valleys and subtropical forests, Azerbaijan can seem like a land forgotten by time. Medieval villages continue to look much the same as they have for untold centuries, a sharp contrast to the high rise buildings and modern architecture blossoming in the cities.

The guide then goes on to list stats—Language: Azeri, literacy rate: 97%. The population, it says, is similar to that of New Jersey, but the land area is roughly ten times that of the same state. I've never been to New Jersey, either, but I guess it must be ten times as crowded as Azerbaijan.

The guys in the front seat are still weighing the pros and cons of their proposed routes, so I flip open the big two-page spread that shows the whole region, from Prague over by my left thumb, to Azerbaijan, which barely escaped being cut off on the right side.

I can see the problem right away.

If you draw a line between Prague and our destination, it would run right through the Black Sea, which is a huge body of water. We'll have to go around it either to the north or the south, but it looks to me like the south, Ram's proposed route, would take us further out of the way, maybe even by hundreds of miles.

So I don't understand why Ram's so determined to go that way. I mean, yeah, we'd avoid the Russians, but what's so important about that? There weren't many Russian girls at Saint Evangeline's, but the few I knew were some of the least snooty people in the student body. So I'm kind of thinking Ion's route would be better.

Nonetheless, Ram insists we head for Slovakia instead of Poland. And for reasons that are even more puzzling to me, especially when you consider Ion has control of the steering wheel, that's the route we take.

South.

Ram's route.

Hundreds of miles out of our way.

Adding long hours—maybe even days—to our trip. And for what? I can't imagine.

But the important thing is, for the first time since my dad dropped me off in Prague, I'm headed home again. So I let that reminder stick in my heart as I settle in to the back seat with Ozzie's bloodied muzzle warm on my lap, and fall into an exhausted sleep.

*

I awake to angry voices and a sickly gray-green sky. It's not just Ram and Ion arguing now. There are men outside the window. Men with guns—big guns.

Instinctively I keep my mouth shut and lower my eyelids to slits, open just far enough so I can see out, not that there's much to see from the back seat. If anybody asks, I'm still asleep.

But just between you and me, I'm watching carefully, wary. Judging by the sky it will be morning soon, but the sun hasn't quite reached the horizon. I don't understand the language Ion and the blokes outside his window are arguing in, but I can tell from the sound of their words they're not getting along very well.

Pretty soon Ion nods, puts the car in gear, and turns us around. The men's voices fade as he cranks his window shut.

"What's that all about?" I ask when Ram glances back toward me.

"We can't go into Romania. Not this way."

Ion scowls. "We could have gone through Ukraine. I could have gotten us through there."

"We'll be fine," Ram states flatly.

"What are we going to do?" I'm sitting up a little straighter now, and my eyes are all the way open. So are Ozzie's.

"We'll go on foot."

"What?"

"All the roads have border crossings," Ion explains. "The border agents won't let us through. The only way into the country is to avoid the border crossing points, which means leaving the road and going through a field or forest on foot, somewhere there's no one to stop us."

"You mean on foot just to cross the border, right? Then we'll find another car, or take a train?"

"We'll go on foot, cross the border in the woods, out of sight. We'll walk." Ram sighs. "As far as we have to."

I remember him saying we wouldn't be able to bring the swords on a train or plane, although I wonder how much that's true. Maybe if we put them in a big duffle bag, or something. But then again, these formerly communist nations are known to be nosy and picky about what makes it into their countries. I don't want to think about what the blokes with the guns would have done if they'd opened the boot and seen our swords.

"Isn't there any other way?"

Ion laughs. "We could try crossing into Bosnia."

He's laughing because the Bosnians are at war with, I think, themselves, and maybe the Herzegovinians or Croatians, or Serbians, or something. I've seen things on the news, usually pictures of burning buildings or bombed out buildings, or people crying because their loved ones were brutally killed.

No, I don't think we're going to go through Bosnia, even if they'd let us through, which I'm starting to doubt.

"Can't we backtrack and go through Russia? I know it's out of the way now, but that would still be faster than legging it."

"Russia is not an option." Ram gives Ion a cold look. Ion is no longer laughing. Something must have passed between them, maybe in the night while I was asleep. I'm curious to know more, but at the same time, I'm picking up a cold vibe and some serious tension between these two, which says now is not the time to probe further.

Ram must know what he's talking about, but it still sounds barmy to me.

"So we're walking to Azerbaijan?" I grab the map and consult the legend in the corner of the two-page spread. It's going to be hundreds, even thousands of miles. I don't know how many miles these guys can walk in a day. Fifty? Maybe a little more? It will take us weeks, even months if we have to contend with mountains and indirect routes. And we're going to be hauling backpacks and swords. "Ozzie's injured. How's she going to walk?"

"Her face is injured," Ram says patiently. "She can still walk."

"But she's old." I say it in a whisper. I don't want to hurt Ozzie's feelings, but she's been old the whole time I've known her, gray around her muzzle and a little stiff in her joints, especially when it's cold.

"I know." Ram whispers, too, his voice resigned. I can hear the echo of all his arguments underpinning those two words — reasons why we shouldn't leave Prague, why it's not safe to attempt the journey, why we should stay and wait for my dad.

But it's too late now for that.

*

My feet hurt.

I was starting to get a blister on my right heel, but Ram put a bandage on it and made me change my socks, which helped the blister, but that doesn't fix the fact that all the muscles in my feet ache. Did you know the human foot has nineteen different muscles in it? (That's one of those 'fun facts' they loved to teach us at Saint Evangeline's.) Times two feet, I have thirty-eight muscles that are killing me, and that's just below my ankles.

Also, my shoulders ache like bruises from hauling my backpack and my swords. I keep trying to shift the weight so it doesn't dig in so badly, but it just shifts back again and hurts worse.

I really hope these guys know where they're going. I'll spare you the details, mostly because I don't want to think about them, but my day has been a blur of forests and fields, barbed wire fences, and bothersome bugs. Mostly mosquitos, with the occasional biting fly.

We've been avoiding villages and farmsteads. For lunch, Ram darted away from me and Ion and Ozzie, and came back a few minutes later with some roasted meat. Even though I don't know how he had time to do it, I'm pretty sure he killed, skinned, gutted and roasted some kind of animal. I didn't ask what kind, but it tasted good.

Other than that, we've just been walking, walking, walking, as the sun slowly rises, peaks, falls, and starts to set.

The Romanian countryside is arguably lovely, but not when you're fleeing with heavy bags. Most concerning of all, Ozzie's having trouble keeping up, and fresh red blood seeps up through her gauze.

I'm afraid this trek is going to be too much for her.

Finally, *finally*, when my feet are so sore they're throbbing and I'm starting to trip over dirt and roots and branches because my feet are half numb from exhaustion, we reach a right thick stretch of woods and Ram and Ion announce it's time to make camp for the night.

I haven't been camping since I was a kid, when we'd head down toward the sea (which I realize now must have been the Caspian Sea). But even then we had things like tents and sleeping bags, food and other gear, which we don't have with us now.

So setting up camp consists of finding a flat stretch of earth big enough to lie down on, clearing away the sticks, and heaping up soft leaves like some kind of mattress.

A mattress with bugs living in it.

I want to go back to Prague.

Except the yagi were there.

Okay, maybe, *maybe*, camping in the Romanian woods is preferable to living at Saint Evangeline's, but I'm assuming these bugs don't bite. If creepy crawly things start chewing on me, this could swing the other way in a hurry.

I can't wait to get off my feet, so as soon as I have a reasonable layer of leaves under me, I sit down and take off my shoes to inspect the damage. Fortunately it looks like the blister on my heel was the only one, and Ram's bandage kept it from getting any worse.

Ozzie settles down beside me nice and close, and I lean my head against her shoulder. She doesn't seem to mind.

Then Ram returns with more roasted meat, which is a bit of a surprise because I didn't even realize he'd stepped away. I thought he was behind my head laying out his leaf bed. We kind of made a triangle — me, Ion, and Ram, with Ion's feet near my feet, and Ram's head near my head, and Ram's feet near Ion's head. I didn't want my head near anybody's feet because, having smelled my own, there's just no way I could willfully lie down like that.

The meat is a different kind this time, and I'm thinking I should ask Ram what it is and how he got it, and how he cooked it so quickly, but I'm too busy chewing, and then I'm full and sleepy and more interested in lying down flat and sleeping than in solving the mysteries of my weird companions.

It's all I can do to stumble to the nearby stream (we've sort of been following this stream — I'm assuming it's a helpful navigational aid in addition to a water source), and I brush my teeth while standing barefoot in the cool water, which is a little numbing but feels absolutely amazing on my thirty-eight sore muscles.

Then I step out and stand on a patch of moss until my feet are dry enough not to track mud back to camp, and I pad back barefoot, and I stretch out on my leaf bed with my Ozzie pillow under my head, and hope none of the unfamiliar noises rustling in the woods are yagi.

Chapter Seven

"Shh, Ilsa, wake up. Don't say anything. Sit up slowly." Ion's voice is a whisper, his face so close to mine I feel his day's growth of stubble scratching near my ear.

Torn by his words from a troubled dream of shadows and yagi and fear, my heart is pounding so loudly I have to strain to hear his instructions.

"Put your shoes on." The stubble around his mouth brushes my ear again now that I've sat up. "We're going to go."

"Go?" I whisper, too, a sound that's hardly more than a breath.

"Yes. You and me — back to the car. We'll drive around via Russia. Ram is crazy but I'm not going to fight him. We'll just sneak away while he's asleep."

The moon is a sliver, and the light that penetrates the canopy of branches is meager, but I find my socks and shoes, and pull them on. My feet aren't so swollen now, but I have no idea what time it is or how long I've slept.

Even as my sleepy hands fumble with my shoelaces, I debate whether going with Ion is the right thing to do. Obviously taking the car is better than walking. Backtracking through the night is better than spending two months hiking through unfamiliar mountains with winter fast approaching. And if we leave Ozzie with Ram, she won't have to endure the journey.

She'll have time to heal.

That, more than anything, makes up my mind for me. I will leave Ram so he can take care of Ozzie instead of escorting me.

I slip into the jacket I was using for a blanket, and start to strap my daggers to my thighs.

"Don't bother." Ion shakes his head, his words mouthed as much as spoken.

I look up at him, blink once, and finish buckling. I'm not sure about leaving Ram. But I *am* sure I'm not leaving my weapons behind. We might be making the rest of the trip in the safety of Ion's Skoda, but Ram taught me how to fight for a reason.

And I'm pretty sure this trip is the reason.

Once I have my swords secure at my hips and across my back (*under* the backpack — they won't be as easy to pull out if I need them, but otherwise they stick out too far and catch on branches) I nod to Ion.

We step away silently. Ram's face is nothing but hair and two lenses reflecting the crescent moon to the sky. Ozzie had shifted out from under my head in the night, and now snoozes closer to Ram. Neither of them moves as we sneak away, which rather surprises me because usually Ozzie is a light sleeper. Then again, given her injuries, I'm surprised she didn't fall asleep on her feet during the trek.

Initially we walk slowly, stealthily, picking our way through the woods so we don't accidentally snap a stick and awaken Ram or Ozzie. But as we get further away from our campsite, we increase our pace.

I also start to wake up a little more, and realize what I'm doing is not a dream. I'm leaving Ram behind. For real.

My dad told me to trust Ram. But the two of them have been keeping secrets from me, which is so very not cool. And Ion gave me a picture of my mother. Ion *wants* to bring me home.

This must be the right choice.

I stumble on. It's difficult in the darkness when there isn't a clear path. I'm grateful for my jeans, which are thick enough to protect my legs from all but the thickest and pointiest branches.

Ion is moving briskly, almost at a jog. Obviously, if we're going to stay ahead of Ram (who's not going to just roll over and go back to sleep if he wakes up and realizes I'm missing) we're going to have to move fast, at least until we get to the car.

If we can reach the car, there will be no way Ram will be able to catch us. We walked all day. If we run most of the night, it won't take us that long to get to the car. How many days will it take to drive home through Russia? A few maybe, depending on how much we sleep. I don't have much experience driving, but driving instruction was part of the curriculum at Saint Evangeline's, and I have my license. I can take a turn driving so Ion can sleep.

I could be home by the end of the week.

The thought pushes me forward, and I run faster, leaping the smaller branches, pounding through the underbrush, panting hard.

And then I smell it.

At first I assume it's the odor of a nearby farm with a lot of livestock. Or maybe I'm crunching some odoriferous leaves as I bound through the forest.

But I sniff harder, inhaling specifically through my nose. It's faint at first, and I think maybe I'm paranoid, or imagining things, but the further we run, the thicker the smell gets, until there's no denying what it is.

"Ion!" I call out to him, but he doesn't slow down.

He's been pulling ahead of me, never mind that I've been running faster and faster, until my throat burns with bile, which mixes with the stink of the yagi, so thick I could choke.

Ion doesn't answer, only runs faster.

I don't want to yell, or do anything to draw any more attention to myself than I've already done by crashing through the dark woods. You know, just in case the yagi haven't noticed me yet.

Right.

"Ion!" I practically scream his name.

He glances back.

Okay, two weird things. One, he's finally taken off his sunglasses, which he'd been wearing all night (I guess I sort of figured they were prescription? Honestly, his eyewear has been the least of my concerns) and his eyes are sort of glowing a silvery green, which would be right lovely if it wasn't completely unnatural.

It's like they're lit up from behind, a little like how cat's eyes glow at night, except *more*. It's freaking me out.

The other thing, which only serves to make the first thing a ba-zillion times more freaky, is that he's grinning.

Not a friendly grin.

More like an evil, mocking, hungry grin.

Yes, *hungry*.

I see this all in an instant, in way less time than it takes to tell it. At the same time, I'm still running and staring at Ion, so of course you can guess what happens next.

I trip over a branch and stumble forward, skidding along the undergrowth (I really hope there's no poison ivy here, because I've had that before and it was awful) and kind of rolling onto my back as these unnatural clacking noises clatter all around me.

Something is moving toward me through the woods. Moonlight glints off squat, domed heads. I can't see them terribly well in the darkness, but what I can see looks like bugs walking upright, except they're taller than I am, and they're making the most horrendous rasping sound, kind of like they're clearing their throats preparing to spit.

Yagi.

They're coming from every direction.

"Ion!" I scream again, this time not so much calling out his name, as just screaming.

The moon is still just a sliver, the light mostly shadow and darkness, but I can see their shiny heads pouring from the trees on all sides, closing in on me. The smell is thick, so thick.

I am completely surrounded.

The rasping sound is seriously freaking me out. I'm pretty much just screaming back at them now, a battle for volume I can't begin to win. Their noise is unearthly, grating, making me clench my teeth together, locking all my joints as I lie frozen on the ground, rendered immobile by that hideous sound.

The simmering moonlight moves in ripples off their heads, highlighting what it had at first camouflaged. Atop their domed heads, what first looked like eyebrows now spring up straight from their heads like spears. Antenna? Horns? The first of the yagi dip their heads toward me, swinging the spears like swords to slice, jab, or impale.

My swords are digging into my back, a sharp, stabbing sensation that pierces my terror and reminds me that I have swords.

I have swords! The reminder is enough to jolt me out

of my sound-induced stupor. Leaping to my feet, I grab my two longest and baddest swords, the ones I keep in the double baldrics in an "x" across my back. I'm hoping they'll do that reassuring singing thing when I pull them out, the resonating hum of metal on metal that ought to send a chill running down the enemy's spine, and maybe even overpower their unearthly grating hiss.

But they don't. My backpack is in the way and my arms are weak and trembley from fear and exhaustion (seriously, what time is it, anyway? Shouldn't the sun come up so I can at least see what I'm doing?). So one sword sort of clatters from its sheath and the other sticks halfway out and I have to give it a couple of extra tugs, during which time the first of the yagi pounce, charging at me like angry insect bulls, horns down, ready to skewer me.

The one free sword is in my left hand, my dominant hand (because I wasn't weird enough already, I guess), and I swing it fiercely toward the two approaching creatures while I pull the other sword free with a final tug.

Theoretically—and this actually worked a bunch of times when I was fighting beef carcasses, which in addition to standing still and not fighting back, don't even have skin to resist my blades—the swing of my sword should have decapitated the yagi.

You know, that whole defending-myself-against-my-enemies-with-such-effective-swordwork-my-blade-never-touches-theirs thing that sounded so good in the meat locker.

Now it sounds utterly naïve.

Because I haven't decapitated anything. My blades deflected their horns, which is helpful insofar as I have not been impaled, but that's all I've accomplished.

I'm not even sure where the yagi's heads are, or if they even have heads, or just those rapier-like spears sticking out from the bulge of their shoulders. I just know, in spite of the darkness, that I have not decapitated them, because I know how my blades feel in my hands when I've sliced through something, or when I've missed entirely and gone swinging around in a circle, nearly tripping over myself in the darkness, which would very nearly have been what happened now, had it not been for the twanging ping against their antennae spears.

Not that I really *missed*. I mean, I swung in the direction I wanted to swing. It's just that, unlike dead cow carcasses, yagi can duck.

Okay, learning curve. I can do this.

I have to. It's not as though I have any choice.

I face the nearest grating noises and swing my blades again. If nothing else, I'll just keep swinging so the creepy creatures stay at arms' length, because I do *not* want them touching me, or running me through with their antennae, or making me freeze up again with that grating noise (they're still making the grating noise, it's just that as long as I keep moving, it doesn't seem to overpower me).

With this swing, I make contact, but instead of a satisfying slicing sensation resonating through my swords, I feel the wrenching twist of a glancing blow.

What, are these guys armored? Seriously, it's like they're steel-plated, or something.

"Ion!" I scream his name again, desperate for him to help me, and angry at him for not keeping me safe.

Ram always kept me safe.

Maybe I shouldn't have left Ram.

The thought of Ram reminds me, not so much on a

conscious level, but in a muscle-memory sort of way, of the butterfly stroke maneuver he taught me — could that have only been yesterday?

I pull my shoulders back and straighten, executing the move, both blades simultaneously, just as he taught me.

I'm not really aiming, just trying to keep my swords moving to keep the yagi away, to deflect their horns, but they're close enough now, practically swarming me, that my sword hits one somewhere about the shoulder.

The blade glances against the armor, but not like before. No, this time the movement — drawing both blades in, together and toward me — pulls the blade flat and swift alongside the armor, inward, toward the yagi's neck, slicing his head clean off.

The fact that I actually got something right is a shock to me, and might have been enough to make me stand still and stare, except thankfully, that muscle memory thing has combined with the serious levels of adrenaline that are searing through me right now, and I don't pause or falter or anything. I just keep swinging.

Which is probably good because I have a sense that if I stop moving for too long, that dreadful sound they're making will freeze my muscles rigid and lock my joints in place, which in addition to being a ghastly feeling, would also make me easy prey for their horns and talons.

So I swing my swords like I'm cutting an endless supply of ribeyes.

Yagi heads are falling everywhere. I bound forward, past two bodies as they fall, trying to get away from the slippery, smooth-domed heads that are rolling near my feet. They're kind of greasy, too. Instead of blood, they're giving off this oily gunk that evaporates into a vapor that stings my eyes.

I'm moving backward, like I'm doing a backward butterfly stroke, escaping a step or two further with every head I decapitate.

I step free, spin, swing. For one thrilling moment, I think maybe I've got this.

And then I realize there's someone else in the woods with me, crashing through the trees. It's not Ion—last I saw him, he was standing off in the other direction, watching me with that hungry, mocking grin.

Whatever it is that's coming toward me, it's bigger than Ion, bigger than the yagi. Silver moonlight glints off two swords, and an unnatural cry cuts through the darkness, louder even than the wailing yagi, as something huge and angry bounds toward me.

Chapter Eight

I leap away from the screaming swordsman in the direction of more yagi, coming at them before they come at me. I have no choice but to keep slicing, using the move Ram taught me, decapitating yagi as fast as I can, spinning as I go to make sure none of them sneak up behind me and spear me through. Their horns have got to be two feet long, maybe longer—which, granted, isn't quite as long as my swords, and certainly not as long as my reach, arms and swords combined, but they're still insanely sharp and wicked looking.

Amazingly enough, although there had to be at least a dozen of these things, the ones left standing are beginning to be seriously outnumbered by the twitching corpses on the ground.

Now if I can just finish off the rest without tripping and accidentally impaling myself on my own sword.

This would be a lot easier if I had any light to see by. The wailing hiss of the living yagi is getting drowned out by the clatter of the fallen, but I can still hear Ion's laughter. I turn toward it.

The screaming swordsman has stopped screaming and is beheading the last of the yagi. For one disoriented moment, in the darkness, I think it must be Ion, finally helping me.

But it almost looks like Ram. Could he have awakened and tracked us down and come to my aid? I suppose it's possible.

Even as these thoughts register, I lower my exhausted arms and zero in on Ion's laughter.

And something exceedingly freakish is happening. I mean more exceedingly freakish than decapitating yagi in the darkness of the Romanian woods.

Ion's laughter is making him grow, almost like blowing up a balloon. Except, instead of being a bigger, rounder form of Ion, he's changing shape, too.

And sprouting wings.

All of this is suddenly surprisingly visible because that kind of glowing gray-green-silveriness of his eyes is now emanating out of the rest of his body, which has a sort of shiny scaly appearance like a fish — like a lake trout or salmon. Except glowing. With wings.

Ion is turning into a dragon.

By the time I realize it, he's done. He's huge. Two, maybe three times bigger than he was before, but with a longer neck so that if he stretched out, he'd be longer still.

And then his wings, which have so far been poised above his shoulders, unfurl like an opening umbrella. Like a huge, bat-winged umbrella that glows with a silvery sheen, stretching through the woods, higher than the trees.

I'm not dreaming. I promise. It would be a nightmare, anyway, but I'm not asleep. Seriously, my subconscious never comes up with anything this vivid.

The air around me churns as Ion extends himself, straining upward with those massive wings far higher than the trees, beating the air once, twice, three times, and lifting off the ground.

I'm standing there gaping, open mouthed (in my defense, I was sucking in air after an exhausting fight) when I realize Ion is flying toward me. But in the time it takes me to realize it, he's there, his body so big that even as I dive away, all he has to do is extend one taloned leg to reach me. He wraps his clawed toes tight around my torso and plucks me from the ground.

The dragon Ion beats his mighty wings and lifts me up past the trees, high into the air toward the clouds. The woods and fallen yagi disappear from sight in the darkness, and I turn my attention to my predicament, able to think clearly for the first time now that we're free of the sound of wailing yagi and the numbing gas of their vaporous slime.

Okay, I know that it wasn't so very long ago, maybe half an hour at most, that I trusted Ion and followed him willingly through the woods. And I know it's theoretically possible that he is somehow rescuing me, whisking me away to safety, or whatever.

But I really don't believe that's what's happening. Sometime in the last half hour, between his mocking smile, his lack of willingness to help me when I screamed his name, and the way he stayed back while the yagi nearly overwhelmed me, I realized that Ion is not on my side. I shouldn't trust him. And I don't want to go wherever he's taking me.

Besides which, I've been afraid of dragons ever since I thought I saw them in the sky the night my village was attacked. So being picked up by a dragon and carried off against my will?

No. I'm not going.

I still have my swords. Maybe I could stab at Ion, or saw through his talons and cut myself free, but we are seriously high in the air right now, probably thousands of feet high, and it doesn't seem prudent to free myself from his grip only to fall to my death.

So I'm looking around frantically, trying to figure out what to do, when I notice a blue streak rising up from the woods, shooting toward us like a bolt from the proverbial blue, whatever that is.

The speeding bolt shoots toward us, growing in size until I can see it's another dragon, similar to the one that's holding me, only with scaly skin that glows sapphire blue. Its wingspan is about the same as Ion's but it's burlier and kind of studly, insofar as a dragon can be studly.

The blue dragon doesn't slow down as he nears us, but barrels into Ion with enough force to knock him off his flight trajectory. We're tumbling through the air, out of control, and even though I don't really want Ion to carry me off through the sky, I'm holding on to his claws for dear life.

The talons around me tighten their grip as Ion and the blue dragon wrestle in the sky. Ion's scraping at the blue dragon with his free talons, holding me up close to his body as he beats at his enemy's face with his wings, screaming like an eagle and spitting fire.

Yes, fire.

Okay, I know mythological dragons were often said to breathe fire, and all, but honestly, the fire takes me more by surprise than flying, never mind that I saw it in the sky above my village a decade ago. That, and the fire is blasted hot, the flame white hot as it emerges from his mouth.

And the blue dragon, of course, breathes fire right back, but he seems to be taking care to avoid hitting me. I appreciate that.

The blue dragon swipes at Ion with his taloned claws and then, without even so much as a twitch of warning to tell me to hang on tight again (I'd let go since he was squeezing me so hard), Ion whirls forward, snapping his talons toward the ground and flinging me toward the earth.

I am plummeting toward the trees below at a speed that's much faster than a simple drop from the sky. Ion flung me with enough force I might worry about whiplash, if I wasn't vastly more concerned about how fast I'm heading toward the hard ground.

My body spins as it falls, and for an instant I look up. The blue dragon is trying to fly downward toward me, but Ion is fighting him, pulling him back, blowing fire in his face as he strains to fly downward, towing Ion through the sky.

Then my body spins again, and I can see the woods, the trees, the path of the creek we were following. I wonder if it would do me any good to angle my body toward the creek, to try to land in the water. But it wasn't that deep, and it had rocks in the bottom. Maybe I could fall in a pile of leaves, but I don't know how to maneuver as I fall through the sky, and the treetops are zooming closer, a blink away.

The air whooshes from my lungs as talons suddenly grip me, gliding with me, forward instead of down, and then swooping slightly upward before sinking again, depositing me gently among boulders so big I can hide between them, out of Ion's reach.

The blue dragon barely pauses before swooping off to the sky again, but he glances back, the briefest of glances, and yet his eyes lock on mine.

Blue. Sapphire blue and glowing.

And then he's gone, shooting toward Ion, meeting him in the sky, continuing the fight.

In that tiny glance, millisecond though it was, I recognized him.

The blue dragon is Ram.

Don't ask me how I know this. It's not like I could possibly recognize him. I've never even seen Ram's eyes before, and obviously the rest of him is completely different. But he looked at me, and the same way I could read his expressions from the twitch of his nose or the angle of his head, I could read this look. He was saying, "Stay hidden. Stay safe."

So I shrink down between the boulders, tucking myself into a rocky nest of safety, leaning back so I can watch the battle in the sky.

They're breathing some serious fire now, Ram especially, and I feel proud of him, and worried for his safety, and guilty about running away, all at once. Not that he should really blame me for running away. Obviously he was keeping some right hefty secrets from me, like the fact that those slicing moves were more about killing yagi than cutting steaks.

And, oh yeah, that he's a dragon.

Ram and Ion tumble through the sky, clawing at each other, pulling back and barreling into each other, breathing searing fire and snapping with sharp teeth. I'm so focused on watching them, rooting for Ram, that I don't hear the approaching noise until it's really close.

Something is out there, in the woods just beyond my boulder. I sniff the air. Yagi? It's hard to say. Their smell is still clinging to me from the battle, but I don't hear the wailing sound from before. Then again, they didn't make that sound until they were upon me, ready to pounce. I almost hope it *is* yagi, because I at least know how to fight them. Otherwise it could be a dragon, or some other fearsome creature I haven't yet encountered.

I grip my swords—yes, I still have them—I got that much right—and peer past the boulders, trying to catch a glimpse of whatever is headed my way. But it's dark down here, particularly dark. There is only shadow and deeper shadow.

The fighting dragons swoop low, breathing fire, and the glow of their flames illumine the woods for an instant.

"Ozzie!" I reach for her, and guided by the flash of dragon fire, she bounds toward me, barreling her shoulders into my legs in a hug that protects her face.

I crumple toward the ground, hugging her, holding her so tight, so grateful for the comfort of her warm furriness, so glad she's okay, and that she found me.

How long I hold her, burying my face in her fur and choking out post-traumatic sobs, I'm not sure, but when I look up again and blink skyward, I can no longer see the dragons.

Where did they go? Did they fly off fighting? Did they kill each other off? Is Ram lying in the woods somewhere, hurting and bleeding and dying?

I really hope not.

"What should we do?" I ask Ozzie. "Should we find Ram?"

Ozzie only lowers herself down into the narrow stretch of soft earth between the boulders. I crouch beside her, and she places her head on my knee.

"What about Ram? Do you think he's going to be okay?"

Ozzie exhales audibly, as if in answer to my question, but I don't speak mastiff, and I don't know what she means. Is she reminding me that Ram is pretty close to invincible, and a dragon besides? Or is she saying she's tired, and we're not going to gain anything by tromping through the woods in the darkness looking for him?

Or is she reminding me of what Ram's look said? *Stay hidden, stay safe.*

Maybe she's trying to suggest, in her gentle, patient way, that I've already rebelled from Ram's instructions enough, and that maybe I should actually trust him, since my father told me to trust him, and since I nearly got us all killed by running away.

So I slump down on the dirt beside her and try to get comfortable, with my legs stretched out in front of me and my back against a boulder—which thankfully, in spite of being hard, is at least sloped at an angle that makes it decent to lean against. And Ozzie puts her head on my lap, kind of like she did in the car, a little like a blanket, which is nice because I need the warmth.

And I close my eyes and wonder. Does my dad know Ram is a dragon? Is that why my dad hired Ram to keep me safe? He must know, right? That dragons are real, that they might come after me, that the only way to keep me safe was to give me a bodyguard every bit as strong and scary as the blokes who are after me.

Obviously Ion isn't trustworthy. The way he flung me down like he wanted to smash me into infinite bits, and then dragged Ram backward to keep him from rescuing me, is a strong indicator that Ion is not trustworthy.

Did my father know that? Or did my father even send Ion?

Years ago, when I was about twelve years old, some of the other girls at Saint Evangeline's were putting pictures of their mothers above their beds, and I wrote to my dad asking for a picture of my mother.

He told me he didn't have one.

I'd forgotten that. Maybe, if I hadn't been so swept away by finally seeing a picture of my mother, and so surprised that she actually looked like me, I would have remembered. My dad keeps a lot of secrets from me, yes, but he doesn't lie to me. Not that I know of, anyway.

In retrospect, I don't think my dad sent Ion. And I think Ram suspected that, but couldn't prove it. He obviously knew Ion and probably knew they were both dragons.

Which brings up the next obvious question: why is a dragon after me, anyway?

Chapter Nine

When the sun rises high enough in the sky to reach past the boulders and warm my face, I awaken, sore and disoriented.

Ozzie is on my lap. The bandages around her nose have worked themselves loose at some point, and I can peek at some of the injuries below. They're scabbed over, not actively bleeding. I might be able to remove the gauze, but I'll wait until she wakes up. She needs her rest.

I lift my head slowly, easing out the kinks from sleeping in an awkward, slumped position. For the first time I realize we're not alone. There's a hand on Ozzie's back, half-buried in her fur, and I look up, past the arm, the leather jacket, the thick black beard, to the face.

Ram's face.

He's sleeping. His eyes are closed, but his goggles are gone.

I have never seen him without his goggles.

Maybe it's because everybody looks angelic when they sleep, even massive bearded swordsmen, but I can't help thinking, bloody bollocks, who knew? Ram is a good looking guy. At least the top half of his face, the part not covered by the beard, is good looking. With his eyes closed, anyway.

I'm probably staring at him, but I'm still sort of groggy from sleep, and it's weird, you know, after working alongside him all summer, to finally see his face…at least the top half.

As I'd suspected, he doesn't show any sign of wrinkles, not even around his eyes, where people even as young as their twenties usually start to get crows' feet.

Is he any older than I am?

He has to be, right? I mean, he knows so much about butchering and how to get back to my home.

Or maybe it only seems like he knows so much, because I know so little, because my father and Ram have refused to tell me anything. Maybe he's not hardly any older than I am.

Suddenly I feel self-conscious and nervous. Ram is a *guy*, not just a talking beard with swords. He's a cute guy, even.

This could be awkward.

I slowly ease myself up so I'm not slumping quite so much, and I flex my toes, forcing the blood through my tired legs to my feet, thinking frantically as I tell myself not to feel nervous. I mean, Ram is still Ram. He's still the same chap I've been working with all summer long.

In some ways, I'm more shocked by his attractiveness than by the fact he's a dragon.

The dragon thing, after all, is so completely out there, so beyond anything I've ever experienced, that it's like I don't even know how to process it.

But a hot guy is something I've actually encountered before, not that I've ever really spoken to one. It's something I've thought about, dreamt about, wished for.

I'm watching his face, telling myself to stay calm, to play it cool, breathing in and out in a soothing, stable manner. And I think I can do this. I can. I was just taken aback for a moment there, more surprised than anything. I'm totally over it. Acclimated to his cuteness completely.

It is no big deal.

Ram opens his eyes and looks at me. "Hey."

My mouth falls open. I can feel it hanging there, and

I'm vaguely aware that I should be saying something coherent instead of the extended "um" noise I can hear coming from myself yet am powerless to control.

His eyes are sapphire blue. Blue like the dragon from last night, the one who saved me and set me down so gently. Remember how I said he was good-looking and cute, sleeping there with his eyes closed?

With his eyes open he is, blimey, wow, I no longer possess the ability to speak.

"Are you okay?" Ram's nose crinkles with concern. It's a familiar sight. I mean, I know this nose. I've held entire conversations with this man that consisted solely of grunts and nose crinkles.

But there are eyes above the nose now, instead of goggles. Wowza blue hotness eyes that look at me like he's afraid maybe the fall through the air hurt me more than he'd realized.

I shake my head to clear my thoughts. "Sorry. I just woke up." I swallow and wet my lips with my tongue. I can do this. Talking. I have been talking to this man, even arguing with him, for the last four months. I can do this.

"You have eyes."

He smiles.

I've got to say, I'm thankful for the beard. At the same time, I'm sort of curious about what he would look like without the beard, but if the rest of his face is half as good looking as the parts I can see, I would be reduced to a pathetic blubbering lump.

Keep in mind, I have zero experience with guys. Especially hot guys with sapphire eyes, who can fly.

But the smiling thing is encouraging, because he could be really upset with me for running away last night and nearly getting myself killed.

I look down at Ozzie's muzzle and try to compose myself. "Do you think we should take the gauze off Ozzie?" I ask without looking up. Conversation is easier if I pretend nothing has changed.

"Maybe after she wakes up. She needs her rest."

"That's what I was thinking." I nod and look up and — still handsome.

Ram isn't smiling anymore. He actually looks almost sad. "Last night…"

His sentence fades to a sigh, and as I stare at his face, waiting for him to say more, I realize something. Maybe part of the reason why Ram is always so silent is because talking is difficult for him. Not physically difficult, but just something he isn't used to doing, or feels inadequate doing, or something like that.

And then I realize maybe the reason why I've only just now figured that out, is because Ram is better at communicating with his face and his eyes, nonverbally, and now that I can actually see more of his face, I understand him better.

That thought gives me the courage to say the difficult words, the confession I didn't want to make. "Ion told me to run away and leave you. He said we could backtrack to the car and drive north through Russia."

"You went with him *willingly*?" He winces, almost like I've punched him.

"I didn't know who he was! I don't even know who you are. Who are you? What are you?"

"We're dragons."

All I can do is stare at his eyes as I absorb this fact, even though, obviously I saw Ram and Ion fighting in the sky last night. I know they're dragons. But it's different hearing him confess it in the light of day.

Ram continues, "The yagi who've been after you are dragon hunters. I know stories and myths have made dragon hunters out to be the good guys, but the yagi aren't good. They don't even have souls. They're a crossbreed between roaches and mercenary soldiers who were captured as prisoners of war."

"Roaches and humans? How is that possible?"

"Dark magic. The yagi were created in a lab during World War II. I've heard about the gruesome experiments, of the way they're hatched and trained. They're bred for a single goal—to destroy us."

"But Ion is a dragon." I'm watching Ram's face for the answer, half expecting to see it there before I hear the words, but all I see is apology and sadness. "Last night, it was like he led me to the yagi. Like he brought me out into the woods and handed me over to them."

Ram nods, slowly. "I was afraid of that. I have known Ion for many years. Because he is one of us, I've been willing to believe him when he claims to be on our side, but I don't trust him. He has betrayed my trust too many times."

"Why didn't you warn me?"

"You were already scared. I didn't want to frighten you more. Besides, he claimed your father sent him. He had a picture of your mother."

"If it even *was* a picture of my mother—"

"It was your mother."

"How do you know? Just because it looks like me—"

"I've met your mother. I helped your father escape after she died."

"Escape?" I'm sincerely confused now. I've never understood the details of my parents' relationship or even how or where I was born. Everything I've been told is only confusing. And didn't I just decide Ram isn't much older than I am? But if he helped my dad when my mom died, and my mom died before I was born...

My agitation has awakened Ozzie, whose bandage shifts even more when she looks up at me with concern, clearly wondering why I'm upset.

And I realize a bunch of things at once. One, we should probably get going. If the yagi are going to come after us again, they could easily stumble across us without even searching too hard. And two, we need to take care of Ozzie's bandages before she tries to remove them herself.

I ease myself to my feet and Ram stands, too. He has his bag and swords and all our stuff, like maybe he went back for them after he fought Ion off. "If you'll hold Ozzie's head still, I'll cut off the bandages." He pulls a dagger from the sheath strapped to his thigh.

So I do my best to hold Ozzie's head still, to comfort her, even though, to be honest, I'm as much comforted *by* her as anything. My world has been shaken, and I have a feeling that before all my questions are answered, it's going to quake even more.

Ram cuts the bandage away, then turns to the side and folds the gauze while I stare at Ozzie's head and hurt for her.

It may have stopped bleeding, but I can't say Ozzie's injuries are healing. Tucked away, out of sight under the bandage, the wounds were festering. The skin looks red and swollen under her fur, and yellow pus oozes from the sores.

It doesn't smell good, either.

"Ram?"

He turns, meets my eyes, looks down at Ozzie's head

when I look that way with alarm. Then he sucks in a breath made audible by concern.

"Is it infected?" I ask, hoping maybe we can splash some alcohol on there and everything will be fine.

But Ram shakes his head. "I've heard yagi may have poisonous venom."

"Venom? On top of everything else?" I'm trying to compile a mental list of everything these nasty creatures have going for them, but I don't even know where to start. "Maybe you should tell me what else they have, before I have to fight them again. I'm lucky I wasn't killed last night. I didn't even know what to do. They were making that hideous noise—it was like they froze me in place with that sound."

"That's one of their defense mechanisms," Ram acknowledges. "They have a paralyzing hiss. The sound waves literally cause muscle fibers and bone to lock up. But as long as you keep moving, they have no power over you."

"That would have been really helpful to know ahead of time." I feel like I'm going to puke from the memory of their shrill screams, the paralyzing sensation it caused in me, and the stink. Oh, that awful stink.

"I thought I'd be at your side to protect you at all times," Ram explains. "I didn't expect you to run away from me."

"I'm not planning to run away again. But could you still tell me what I'm up against? The venom? Where does that come from? The horns on their heads?"

"No, the horns on their heads are as sharp as any blade. They can skewer you, but they don't excrete venom. I was hoping that's what got Ozzie, but obviously I was wrong. The venom comes from the spikes on their arms and legs. They have to get pretty close to use it. Most often they'll get you with their horns or their talons, first. Their talons are like rows of slicing fingers. Very nasty."

"Is that all?" I try to sound as though I'm not completely overwhelmed. Maybe it's a good thing I didn't know all this about them ahead of time, or I might have been too frightened to fight.

Ram shrugs. "Also, their blood is thick and oily and contains a neurotoxin chemical that produces a numbing, stinging sensation wherever it touches you—a bit like nettles. Not enough to kill a person, but not pleasant, either. When their blood makes contact with the air, such as when they're decapitated, it vaporizes into a gas that can sting your eyes, and even becomes hallucinogenic if you inhale large quantities."

"How bizarre."

"Many of these traits and defenses come from the cockroaches they're bred from, just on a much larger scale."

I've got my eyes closed as I absorb all this information. I thought the yagi were creepy enough before I knew about them. Still, I'm sure I'm better off knowing what I'm up against. And I'm relieved I wasn't hurt last night, in spite of my ignorance. "I'm glad I kept them at bay with my swords. And then you showed up. How did you know, anyway?"

"Ozzie woke me up. She picked up your trail from the smell, otherwise I don't know if I would have found you in time."

"Good Ozzie, good girl." I scratch her behind her ears, being careful not to disturb the oozing gashes. I ask Ram, "What can we do for her?"

He looks down at the festering wounds and I see that look on his face, that mixture of sadness and apology that I already know too well. "Maybe your dad will have a solution. Let's get you home."

"How? We don't have a car. The car was Ion's. I looked at the map yesterday. It's over two thousand miles to Azerbaijan from Prague. Where are we, anyway? Somewhere in western Romania? It's going to take us weeks to walk there." I look down at Ozzie's head emphatically. She needs help. Soon. And I really don't think walking that far is going to help her condition.

"We can walk." Caution slows Ram's words. "Or we can fly."

"Like in a plane? Do you think they'll let us on with the dog and our swords?"

"I mean, *fly*. Like I did last night."

"And what, then? You'll carry both me and Ozzie?"

"I can carry Ozzie." He meets my eyes again, this time holding my gaze and not letting go, as though he's trying to communicate something very important, or gauge my understanding of something, but whatever it is, I have no idea. I stare back at him blankly, really not getting it.

"What about me?"

"I don't know. It's a long way for your first flight, but we could take it in stages."

More confused than ever, I remind him, "I flew with Ion last night. It wasn't that bad. If it means getting home I can hang on longer, I'm just not sure how comfortable Ozzie will be. Are you sure you can carry both of us?"

The whole time I'm talking, he's looking at me, his eyes sparkling with a kind of inner light, his gaze patient yet probing. My hands are still behind Ozzie's ears as she leans her head against my leg, and Ram puts one hand on mine.

I'm instantly aware of his touch. It's comforting. Gentle. Strong.

Blast it, I fancy him.

He doesn't look away from my face. "Do you know why the yagi were after you?"

Everything from the way he's touching my hand to the patience behind his words says there's something big here, something monumental. "I don't know. If they're dragon hunters, that's really weird that they'd come after me." I swallow the last word as reality hits me.

I wish Ram would stop looking so bloody apologetic. "Ilsa? You're a dragon."

Chapter Ten

In retrospect I feel daft for not making the connection sooner, but in my defense, I didn't know dragons were real until last night, and even then, I was more wrapped up with trying to survive than any existential self-examination. Also, I guess part of me assumed that's one of those things a person ought to know about themselves before they're eighteen years old and being stalked by dragon hunters across the wilds of Romania.

And to be honest, it takes a while for the truth to sink in, especially since I'm simultaneously trying to ignore my unexpected feelings of attraction to Ram. "I'm a dragon?"

"Yes."

"I'm a person."

"Yes."

"I mean, I'm not a dragon. I can't be a dragon because I am a person."

Ram turns his head a little to the side in that way he does when he knows I'm denying the obvious truth.

I told you he's way better with non-verbal communication than words.

And I get it. "You look like a person, but you can change into a dragon."

He nods.

"I can change into a dragon?" I'm tempted to point out that's madness, but to be honest, it's no crazier than the fact dragons exist at all. Sure, why not? And I can breathe fire. Of bloody course I can.

"Yes."

"How do you know? Have you seen me do it?" I'm challenging him now, because I don't right well want to be a dragon. And it's not so much that I don't *want* to be a dragon, as that I find the idea of being a dragon utterly repellant. As we fled for the caves when I was eight, running and screaming, terrified, in the dark of night, I saw dragons flying overhead.

Ever since, I've told myself that it wasn't real, that I'd imagined it or misinterpreted what I'd seen, but now I know I really did see dragons flying in the night sky above our village, fighting and breathing fire. But in all those years, even though I told myself it wasn't real, I still hated the dragons. The dragons chased me from my home. The dragons sent me into hiding and exile. Real or not, that was my earliest association, and the one that still stands today.

I don't want to be one of those thieves of childhood, one of those enemies of peace.

So I'm resisting Ram's announcement, challenging it with all the opposition of a terrified eight year old. "How do you know I'm a dragon if no one's ever seen me be a dragon?"

"You've never taken on dragon form, but your parents were both dragons. Once you change for the first time, your eyes will become jewel-toned."

"That's why you wear goggles all the time, and why Ion wore sunglasses, even at night." It's easier for me to talk about the eyes than the whole dragon thing.

"Yes."

"So I'll have to hide my eyes all the time."

"Only when you're around people who don't know who you are. Once we reach your village, you'll be safe."

Slowly, a bunch of things that never made sense

about my life, and never seemed fair, start to click into place—not that I accept or embrace them—far from it. But on a purely intellectual level, they make sense. Now I know why I smelled yagi when I was eight. And I realize something else. I'd heard their wailing then, too, but distantly, and assumed it was a warning siren. I'd attributed the paralyzing effect to my own fear. But maybe I wasn't as much a coward as I've always assumed. "When the village was attacked, right before my father took me away to Saint Evangeline's…"

"They were looking for you." Ram squeezes my hand, and I squeeze back. "That's why your dad took you to Saint Evangeline's—to keep you safe."

"And to keep the village safe."

Ram dips his head, one of those almost-a-bow gestures like Ion gave him at the butcher shop. "True. They had no reason to attack once you were gone."

"No reason? Why are they after *me*, specifically?"

Ram draws a deep breath and looks up.

I remember that we don't have the luxury of standing around. Sure, I have plenty of questions, but we need to keep moving before the yagi catch up to me. "We should get going. Do you really think I should try to fly?"

Ram sucks in a deep breath. "Right now? No. Not in the daylight. We'll be seen. I try never to fly in daylight, not unless I'm over the ocean or somewhere equally remote."

It's not until I let out a relieved breath that I realize how much I didn't want to try flying—especially not after Ion flung me through the air last night. The thought of taking to the air makes my stomach lurch. And besides, I have so many questions. I doubt Ram could answer them in dragon form.

"Let's get walking, shall we?" Ram suggests. He leads me out from between the boulders, which were near the top of a hill. From here we can see far, and Ram scans the area, his brow furrowed. "We'll have to give wide berth to the places we encountered yagi yesterday."

"We killed them."

"We killed the ones who attacked us. In my experience there are always more."

I scan the horizon, too, aware that the dragon hunters could leap out at us at any time, that they may have been tracking us down all night while we slept. "What do they look like? I've only ever seen them in darkness."

"They look a lot like people, at least from a distance. The yagi keep their antennae flat against their heads. The antennae are flexible when they want them to be, but they go rigid like rapiers when the yagi fight. Generally they try to cover up so you can't see that their heads are small, inhuman, and flat, and to hide their exoskeleton. In cities they wear trench coats and fedoras." Ram appears to be satisfied that no yagi are lurking anywhere too close, and he picks a path down the hill, watching Ozzie as she lumbers after him. At least her injuries don't seem to be causing her too much pain—for now.

"Exoskeleton, huh? That explains it. I thought they seemed armored."

"Precisely. They have a smooth, hard shell all over their bodies. It's usually a coppery brown, like the roaches they're descended from. It's also bullet-proof, which is why swords are so much more effective against them than guns. In fact, shooting at them can be very dangerous. Bullets can bounce off in any direction. It's not safe to fire a gun at them."

I fall into step beside Ram so we can speak without

being too loud. I don't want to draw unnecessary attention our way, but at the same time, I need to know as much as I can learn about my enemy. "So, when I decapitated them…"

"Their exoskeletons are jointed, almost like an armadillo's body, but most of the joints overlap so you can't pierce their armor—the only exception is at the base of their heads. They really don't have much of a neck. The seam is narrow, but in order for them to turn their heads to the sides, the joint isn't completely covered. You have to hit it just right."

"But you taught me how."

Ram pauses and grins at me. "I'm glad you got the hang of it. I tracked you down last night thinking I needed to rescue you, but you had things under control."

I'm glad Ram doesn't realize how close I'd come to not having things under control at all. The sun is warm on my face. That, or I might be blushing slightly. I keep walking, half a step in front of Ram so he can't see the red on my cheeks. "Until Ion picked me up."

"It's a good thing I got there when I did."

While technically his statement is correct, I can't help feeling insanely frustrated by the situation. "If I'd known I couldn't trust him, I wouldn't have gone with him in the first place." I try to keep my voice calm, but the undercurrent of anger is so close to the surface I can hear it in spite of my best efforts.

"I told you already—I didn't know whether Ion was trustworthy or not. You knew he and I had been butting heads. You knew everything you needed to know."

"Except for the part where I'm a dragon and the yagi are after me." It's all I can do to keep my volume under control. I don't want to alert the yagi to our presence with my shouting. So I don't shout. But neither am I calm.

"You knew the yagi were after you."

"But I didn't know why, or what they are. I still don't know why they're after me."

"They're dragon hunters. You're a dragon."

"But why me? Why not everybody else in the village?"

"Nobody else in the village is a dragon."

I all but stumble and fall, but when I look at my feet, there's nothing there to trip me up. Ram and Ozzie both pause and look at me with concern.

"I'm the only one?" A weird sense of guilt fills me with overwhelming dread. "Wait a minute, how many dragons are there? There's me and you and Ion."

"And your father."

"Okay." I nod. That makes sense that my dad must be one if I'm one. "Who else?"

"Your mother was a dragon."

We're no longer walking, just standing still in the shaded woods. I don't think I can handle having this conversation and walking at the same time. "Who else?"

"It's hard to say. Long ago, every region on earth, every town, village, and island, had a dragon protector. They kept their people safe from attack. They kept the earth at peace."

"Dragons? You always hear about them fighting—"

"Sometimes they had to, to defend their people. And they're territorial. They don't tend to like other dragons, besides their own family members. But dragons are inherently peaceful." Ram starts walking again, making his own path through the woods, disturbing little. The trees grow thicker and the underbrush more dense as we descend the hill.

"As the years passed, humans discovered they could conquer their neighbors if they killed their dragons. Great military leaders arose, Attila the Hun, Alexander the Great, and many others, who learned they could conquer people by destroying their dragons. The Crusades— remember the crusades? Dragons played a huge role, but they were vilified for protecting their people. The truth of their good deeds was redacted from the history books, changed to make them sound evil. New stories were spread, making them out as a dangerous menace in hopes that people would betray or even kill their own dragons. Those rumors persist to this day.

"Eventually, people realized they had to keep their dragons' identities, even their existence, secret. To claim people were dragons put targets on their heads. Dragons went into hiding. They remain in hiding still."

I absorb Ram's words slowly, their truth made so much more difficult to swallow because he's not talking about mythical figures or even strangers from the pages of history books, but of himself and my father. And me. "That's why the yagi are hunting me?"

"They're bred to destroy all dragons, yes, but you are particularly threatening to them."

"Why?"

Ram almost laughs, but the sound is more one of irony and regret. "Of the names we've just listed—Ion, your father, me—what do we have in common?"

"You all keep secrets from me?"

"Yes," Ram acknowledges, "but more generally? We're all—"

"Guys? Male?"

"Yes. Alone, we are not a threat. We have proven our willingness to keep our heads down and not cause trouble, to stay hidden. But you, on the other hand, you—"

"They think I'm going to cause trouble?" I bound over a fallen log, nearly laughing at the suggestion. The closest I came to causing trouble at Saint Evangeline's was eating chicken bones, and since I mostly kept that a secret, I was never punished.

"Your children might." Ram bounds over the log, as well, landing in front of me and pausing. "You, Ilsa, are a female. And females are very few. I'd like to believe there are more in the world, hiding somewhere, but I've only ever known of three. My own mother, your mother, and Eudora."

"Eudora?" I repeat the name, conscious of the way his voice changed from affection when he spoke of our mothers, to a dreadful chill when he spoke the female dragon's name. "Who is she?"

"Remember when I said the yagi were created in labs?"

"Yes?"

"Eudora oversaw their creation. It was her idea, her mad science—her dark magic that stretched the limits of science. She is the one who trains them and sends them out to hunt us."

"But she's a dragon, too, right?" I'm walking a little faster now, almost as though Eudora or her yagi might come up on us any moment. "Why would she want to kill off the last of her people?"

Ram bounds across another fallen log, letting out a sigh that's almost disgusted. "The short answer? Because she doesn't believe dragons belong in the modern world. She thinks we're the vestigial organs of the earth and should be amputated so the world can move forward.

Dragons, in her mind, pull us backward to a time when wars were fought with blades and fire instead of words. She believes we should all be destroyed, but since the best weapon against a dragon is another dragon, she's taken it upon herself to do the purging."

Ram pauses reflectively before he continues. "But there's more to it. Dragons are territorial creatures who don't get along well with their own kind. They say it's stronger with females, the need to be the alpha, to be the top woman."

Having witnessed the popularity games of dominance many of the girls at Saint Evangeline's played, I understand what he's talking about. "But to kill off everyone?"

"Not everyone. She has a history of making deals with others. From what I understand, she's able to train the yagi using scent, to target specific dragons—such as you—and exempt other dragons, such as herself and presumably Ion. I can only assume Ion is working for her."

"He's a traitor to his own kind?" On a gut level, I'd realized as much the night before, when he led me into the midst of the yagi and then laughed while they swarmed me. "Why would he do that?"

"His reasons are not so different from Eudora's, I imagine." Ram holds out his hand to help me over a fallen log nearly as high as my waist (there are lots of fallen logs, because we aren't following any sort of path that I can see. These woods are thick and old). I am grateful for his gesture, which is more than a simple courtesy. With swords at my back, hips, and thighs, clambering over large obstacles can be tricky. With his help, I climb atop the log, then jump down on the other side.

Ozzie stretches her front paws up the side of the log, then whimpers.

Ram scoops her up, lifting her gently and settling her back on her feet on the other side.

My throat constricts as I watch. Ozzie is getting weaker. I wonder about the poison and how fast it might act, but Ram said he doesn't know much about it. Nor do I suppose that's something a normal doctor or veterinarian would have experience with. No, the only thing we can do is try to get her to my father and hope he knows how to help.

Rather than worry helplessly about Ozzie, I turn Ram back to our conversation. I'm glad he's finally willing to answer my questions, even if his explanations are completely terrifying. At least now I know what we're up against.

"Ion wants to destroy the other dragons so he can be the top dragon?" I clarify.

"Something like that." Ram watches Ozzie as she trudges forward. He's worried about her, too. "Beginning in the enlightenment, there has been a movement among dragons and their people, professing the belief that dragons are a relic of ancient times, made obsolete by humanity's progress. That we're dangerous and unnecessary and evil, and we don't belong in the world anymore."

Sweat drips down my back along with a trickle of dread. If you'd have asked me any time before yesterday whether dragons had a place in our modern world, I'd have said they didn't. In every story I can ever remember, dragons are the enemy, a terrifying source of destruction. And I hate destruction. Ever since my village was attacked and I had to flee for my life, I have hated violence of any kind.

You can't tell me dragons aren't violent creatures. I saw Ram and Ion fighting last night.

Ram shoots me an apologetic glance. "Eudora believes that the earth must be cleansed of the plague of dragons. She's vowed not to rest until we're all dead, and she created the yagi to do her bidding, to track us down so she can destroy us."

I stop still in the woods, not because there's any obstacle before us, but just to look at Ram and digest what he's said.

Eudora wants to kill me simply because of who I am, and who my children might be? It's a terrifying thought, made all the more dreadful because I was nearly overwhelmed by the yagi last night. If Ram hadn't fought Ion, Eudora would have won already.

But at the same time, I understand Eudora's arguments far too well. Having witnessed the fight between Ram and Ion, I've seen how powerful and dangerous dragons can be. So I can't shake the thought that maybe Eudora is right. Maybe dragons don't belong in this world any longer.

The thought settles like a knot in the pit of my stomach along with a realization that makes far too much sense. Perhaps this is why I've never felt like I fit in, not at Saint Evangeline's or in Prague. Because I don't belong in the world at all.

Chapter Eleven

"I'm hungry. You?" Ram changes the subject.

I'm glad he did. I've heard as much as I can handle for now, and to be honest, I *am* hungry. If I can get some food in my stomach, maybe it won't knot up so dreadfully. "Starving."

"Stay here with Ozzie. I'll be right back."

Before I can ask where he's going, he darts away, and I settle my bum onto a low rock to wait, my thoughts spinning.

I am a dinosaur. I am a dragon. I'm a bigger freak than I'd ever suspected, and the yagi are probably justified in wanting to kill me.

Still, I hope the yagi don't show up while I'm sitting here, unprepared, with Ozzie's head on my lap and Ram off to who-knows-where in search of food.

It's not long before I hear rustling in the woods, and I've just gotten my hands around the hilts of my swords when Ram emerges from the trees carrying a headless deer by its hind legs.

The animal is dripping fresh blood and I feel a little sorry for it.

But also hungry.

Seriously, this shouldn't be much different from butchering beef, but it is. Ram uses a hooked dagger to slit the deer's belly, gutting it and peeling back the skin. I try to remind myself that this is where meat comes from—everything from fast food burgers to the steaks I so love. They were all animals at one point.

But the deer, at least until Ram finishes skinning it,

looks more like a loveable woodland creature than a roast.

"Want it cooked, or raw?" Ram asks as he tugs the last of the hide from the dangling legs.

For an instant I'm tempted to tell him I don't want it at all, but my stomach growls, reminding me I'm hungry. And I know I need to keep my strength up if I expect to make the journey home. "Cooked."

Ram holds the venison high above the undergrowth and glances around, stepping clear of some overhanging branches. "Don't want to set the woods on fire," he says with a wink.

And then he does it—the thing I can only assume he's been doing out of my sight before every meal I've ever shared with him.

He breathes fire.

Beautiful, multi-colored fire that emerges blue-tinged and white hot from his mouth, then flickers to yellow and licks the sides of the meat with red and orange flames.

He pauses to suck in a breath, turns the venison so the other side is near him, and breathes fire again. Then he extends the roasted animal toward me. "Grab your sword and lop off what you want."

I do. I'm so hungry, I take a quarter section of the animal and dig in, but even as I'm chewing and swallowing, I feel guilty. This is why I like meat so much, isn't it? This is why I'm a chicken-bone-crunching freak.

Because I'm a dragon.

Ram offers a leg quarter to Ozzie and she opens her mouth to eat, but then winces and sniffs the meat, licking it a few times before looking up at us with sad eyes.

When she finally manages a few nibbles, I glance at Ram and swallow the bite of meat in my mouth.

Ram looks concerned and steps closer, consulting me in low tones. "We could try to rest now, then fly as dragons once night falls."

I can't look at him, but instead hug myself, watching Ozzie, my appetite gone. "I don't know enough to make that choice," I admit. "I don't know how to change or to fly."

What I don't tell him is that I can't imagine turning into a dragon. I don't even think I want to be a dragon. To allow myself to transform into a giant flying lizard—that implies a certain level of acceptance that I just don't feel. As long as I stay human, I can pretend this dragon business isn't about me. But if I become one, even for a night, then that's part of who I am.

"I can help you," Ram offers. "It's not too difficult, but it's not an easy choice. I'm not sure if it's the right choice right now. Changing is exhausting, especially when you're not used to it. I don't know how far you'll be able to fly the first time, and I'd hate to have to put down somewhere even more dangerous than here."

"And didn't you say it would make my eyes change? So it would be harder for me to hide?"

Ram repeats my words, confirming them. "Harder to hide as a person, and when you're in the air, flying as a dragon, you'll be out in the open for anyone to see. There's nowhere to hide in the sky, unless the clouds are just right. But clouds can be trouble, too, because then you can't see where you're going or if something's headed toward you."

I close my eyes as I ponder my options. "I want to get Ozzie to my father as soon as we can. I don't think she'll make it on foot." I glance up at Ram, and he's nodding like he understands. "At the same time, we're still awfully close to where the yagi attacked us last night. I don't know if I'd feel safe staying put. I'm not even tired enough to sleep right now."

"How about we keep moving, then? We can always rest later, or sleep a bit this evening and fly in the deepest darkness before dawn. I doubt you'd be able to fly for more than a few hours your first time, anyway."

I let out a shaky breath and nod. Ram's plan works around some of my biggest misgivings — like that I don't want to be a dragon, or I'm not ready to be one yet, anyway. "But what about Ozzie? Do you think she can keep going?"

At the sound of her name, Ozzie looks up at us, her expression apologetic. She's at least managed to eat some of her meat, but I suspect even that effort has worn her out.

"I can carry her." Ram crouches down and addresses Ozzie. "Ready to go, girl?"

Ozzie thumps her tail, and Ram scoops her up, hoisting her above his shoulders, adjusting the swords on his back so the sheaths function as railings, holding Ozzie in place behind his head. She settles her muzzle onto her paws, and I'm glad Ram has such wide shoulders, and that he's strong enough to carry Ozzie.

Even if I'm not glad he's a dragon.

We walk like that for hours — Ram carrying Ozzie, and me just trying to process everything I've learned. I could ask Ram more questions, but I've already heard more than I want to know, and anyway, I think carrying Ozzie is wearing him out more than he cares to admit. Honestly, the dog probably weighs more than I do. But I also know Ram was tired after his fight with Ion last night. And he'd said it takes a lot of energy to be a dragon, so I'm sure that doesn't help.

The evening is getting cool and the sun is sinking below the treetops when the creek we've been following (not the same creek from the day before — we don't want to make it *easy* for the yagi to track us) empties into a clear lake, and Ram suggests we should rest for a few hours, then maybe try flying.

I'm in favor of the idea, except possibly for the flying part, but since that won't be happening for a few hours at least, I scoop leaves into a comfy bed for Ozzie.

Ram lowers her gently onto the leaves and I get a good look at her for the first time since Ram started carrying her.

I want to cry.

The pus on Ozzie's head has started to bubble and swell in putrid blisters. For the first time I wonder if she'll make it through the night, never mind the trek past the Black Sea.

"Maybe we should start flying now." I look to Ram for guidance.

He, too, appears horrified by the appearance of Ozzie's injuries. But he shakes his head. "We need to rest — we all need to rest. Ozzie won't be up to the flight if she doesn't lie still a bit. Neither will the two of us."

He's right. In my heart, I know he is, though I don't like it. Resigned, I make my bed, eat the fish Ram pulls from the lake, brush my teeth, and lie down, just as the sun begins to set.

*

It's dark when I awaken, but the sliver of moonlight is slightly wider and brighter tonight, enough for me to see the festering gouges on Ozzie's head. Her ribs rise and fall, so I know she's breathing. Her sleep, at least, appears to be undisturbed.

I glance at Ram. He, too, is deep in slumber, exhausted from carrying the heavy dog after fighting Ion as a dragon the night before.

They both need their rest.

Thirsty, I walk the dozen or more yards from our campsite to the lake, past trees and bushes to the rocky shore, where I scoop water into my mouth and then watch my reflection as the droplets from my hands send concentric circles shimmering away in tiny waves.

So, this is the face of a dragon, hmm?

I think of the picture of my mother and wonder what it was like for her, how she managed to fit in at Saint Evangeline's or if she ever did, and whether I should run back and wake up Ram so we can keep going.

For Ozzie's sake, we need to get to my dad as soon as possible. But I'm not sure if I'm ready to change into a dragon, which is kind of a prerequisite for that to happen.

Not that I wouldn't do anything to save Ozzie.

I would. In a heartbeat.

But changing into a dragon? I guess I can't quite comprehend how it's even possible, never mind that I already watched Ion do it.

Leaves rustle behind me and I turn, half expecting to see Ram checking up on me. A man steps from the bushes, but not from the direction of our camp. The silhouette isn't as roach-like as the yagi, nor does this man smell like my enemies.

Faint moonlight shines down in slender beams between the trees. He steps into its silvery light.

"Ion?" I whisper his name. I don't reach for the swords at my back, but I'm glad I thought to put them on before making my trek to the lake. It's not a long walk, but I wanted to be safe.

"Hey, Ilsa." He rakes a hand back through his hair and the moonlight hits his face. His cheekbones are angled upward in a way that accentuates his handsome features, and I can't help wondering if this is a practiced move. "I wanted to apologize for last night."

"Oh? The part where you tried to kill me, or the part where you tried to kill me?" I'm trying to sound confident and snarky, but I'm bluffing. I do not feel confident. In fact, I'd be screaming for Ram if it wasn't for the fact that I'm frightfully curious why Ion would show his face just now. And he *did* apologize.

"I wasn't trying to kill you." Ion steps closer.

"Really?" I flex my fingers, ready to grab for my sword, and sniff the air. I don't smell yagi, but there's a breeze coming off the lake, so that doesn't mean they couldn't be hiding downwind. "You didn't lure me into a swarm of yagi and laugh while they attacked me?"

"I wanted you to see that you could fight them, to know how strong you really are."

"Rubbish."

"You were never in real danger. I didn't let them touch you."

I narrow my eyes as Ion steps closer to me. It's true, the yagi never touched me. But I'm right sure that had more to do with my swordwork than Ion's protection. "And the part where you flung me toward the earth?"

"To keep you out of the fight. Ram was breathing fire."

"So were you."

"But I kept you out of it. On purpose." He's close enough to me now I can see the silver swirling in his gray-green eyes, like mercury pooling, liquid metal. Then he grins that grin that's way too confident. "If I'd wanted to kill you, you'd have been dead long before the yagi showed up. I want to help you, Ilsa, but you need to trust me."

I'm breathing heavily, my whole body tense, staring down Ion and hating the fact that dragons keep telling me to trust them, but none of them have done anything to earn my trust. They keep secrets from me and betray me.

I shake my head. "I trusted you. You had your shot. You blew it."

Ion tips his head to the side. There's something like pity on his face, and I'm tempted to smack him. But his words still my hand. "You don't want to be a dragon, do you, Ilsa?"

I don't answer aloud, but I can feel some of the tension leaving my body. Okay, so he has my attention now. I don't know how he knew that—I could barely admit it to myself—but he knows. And he said he wanted to help me.

He keeps talking, his words smooth. Charming. "You don't have to be a dragon. We can fix that."

"How?"

"The same way we meld soldiers and roaches. The same power that melds life to life can be used to pull life from life. It's in your DNA, in your genes, your blood. We eliminate the dragon bits and keep only the human bits."

I shudder. That doesn't sound safe.

Or wise.

Or comfortable.

Ion's practically purring, his words enticing,

saccharine sweet. "We make you human, only human. You could be a real girl. One who belongs."

I don't trust Ion. I don't. I trusted him last night and that didn't end well.

But at the same time, I want to be human.

I want to belong.

I don't want to be a freak any more.

"Come with me, Ilsa. I only want to help you." Ion stretches out his hand toward me.

I look at his hand.

It looks so normal, so human.

What do I do? My dad told me to trust Ram. Ram told me Ion is not to be trusted. Ion works with Eudora, who made the yagi. That's probably who would make me human—a crazy, mad-scientist dragon woman.

I take a step back, away from Ion, and shake my head. "No."

"Ah, but you will." Ion's words are a whisper pressed tight to my ear as he lunges, wrapping his arms around me in an instant, pinning my arms to my sides so I can't reach my swords, burying my face against his chest so I can't even scream for help.

I struggle to escape Ion's grip, but blimey, he's strong. There's no way I'm going to be able to get my arms up and grab the swords at my back, but the daggers on my thighs aren't so much of a stretch. I wriggle and thrash, tugging my hands toward the hilts until finally my right hand reaches one handle.

Yes, my non-dominant hand, if anyone's keeping track. Obviously not the best choice, but since Ion's got my other arm half-twisted behind my back (it's like he knows that's my best hand), this is as good as it's going to get. And I need to hurry. I don't want him going all dragon on me and carrying me off through the clouds again.

By throwing myself into him, I manage to jar us just enough to wrench the dagger from its sheath. With a flick of my wrist, I stab the spear toward his belly.

Ion freezes. "You wouldn't."

I still can't talk (trust me, if I could talk, I'd have screamed for Ram by now) but I flick my wrist a bit more, jabbing the dagger deeper. I don't think I've broken his skin, or I'd feel a warm gush of blood, assuming dragons bleed. I mean, I bleed when cut, so that doesn't seem like too much to assume.

To be honest, I don't think I can cut him, and I'm not just talking about the moral question of stabbing another human being, even if he is a dragon. I mean I'm pushing the dagger as hard as I can into his belly, but the way we're standing with my arms pinned under his, and given the angle of the blade against his skin, I can't push the blade much further, not without risking losing my hold on it.

And I'm not going to risk that.

So I let the sharp edge of the knife make my point for me, pressing hard, as hard as I can.

Ion isn't squirming. He's very nearly holding his breath, though. I suspect he doesn't dare take a deep breath or the edge of my dagger will puncture his skin. Nor can he attempt to change into a dragon for the same reason—I could do all sorts of damage before he got far enough along to fly off with me.

"I told you I don't want to hurt you," Ion reminds me in a clipped whisper.

I brace my feet against the ground and push toward him. It's not quite the same as digging the knife in, but it gets my point across — that I will stab him if I have to. If I can.

But as he readjusts his stance, the pressure on my face eases ever so slightly, and I manage to turn my head to the side. "Ram! Hel —"

That's all I get before Ion clamps down. "Big mistake," he whispers, then barks an order into the shadows beyond the trees. "Attack!"

Chapter Twelve

The clatter of yagi fills the air, and with a dreadful sinking sensation, I realize Ion was not alone. The only thing restraining him was his hope for my cooperation. He drags me back toward the camp as the yagi pounce on Ram, who's on his feet, swords in hand.

"Let's watch, shall we?" Ion shifts the way he's holding me, so I'm facing outward, forced to watch Ram attempting to defend himself against overwhelming odds, the yagi swarming him so closely he hardly has room to swing his blade.

Horrible.

I can't even try to get free from Ion, because the yagi are making that wailing noise again, paralyzing me. But at the same time, my mouth is now free, and I can talk. Apparently the paralysis-inducing noise can't silence me. I have one burning question I want answered. "Why do you want me alive?"

"Why should I kill you?"

"Wouldn't that be a lot easier?" Even as I'm speaking, yagi hurl themselves at Ram. The moonlight isn't much brighter than the night before, barely enough to see by, but Ram's eyes are glowing a fierce blue, and even from this distance, Ion's eyes give off a faint, silvery glow. So I can see most of the action, and I can tell the yagi are getting uncomfortably close before Ram slashes them away. I wonder about the venom or whatever it is, and cringe at the thought of Ram getting poisoned.

"Easier, yes. Vastly so. But Ilsa, don't you know what you mean to me? Can't you see what you could be to me?" His mouth is close to my ear, his breath heavy, moist against my neck. As he speaks, his hands shift—still holding me tight, clamping my arms to my sides, but now his fingertips press against my waist, grazing my hips, the implication clearer than words. "You and I, Ilsa, we could be the start of a new generation—"

I don't need to hear any more. Ram is barely able to keep the yagi at bay, I can't see Ozzie in the darkness, and Ion's pawing hands have shifted the balance, spurring me into motion in spite of the yagis' freezing wails. I spin free, the dagger in my right hand extended toward Ion's heart as I step back and pull out one sword with my left hand.

Just as quickly, Ion has a sword in his hand.

Blimey.

I leap backward, into the fray. I'd rather fight yagi with Ram than try to match swords with Ion.

For a few moments, all is chaos, the yagi pressing so close I can't see what I'm doing. I whip my left arm—the only one with a sword—in the butterfly maneuver, not even bothering to aim, while I slash and jab with the dagger in my right hand. I don't expect to kill the yagi with the stunted blade. I'm just hoping to keep them from poisoning me with their barbed appendages, spearing me with their horns, or slashing me with their talons.

We're fighting in tight range, nearly overwhelmed. I'm not even sure where Ram is until I feel something bump my back. At the same instant, I hear his voice.

"Keep your back against mine." It's Ram. He has a strategy. I feel a surge of hope. With his swords slashing behind me, I don't have to spin myself dizzy just to keep yagi from sneaking up and spearing me in the back.

I'm swiping with the sword in my left hand, the way he taught me. Now that he's at my back, I have a chance to slip the dagger back into the sheath on my thigh, and pull out my other long sword, the metal singing as it should.

The hybrid henchmen fall back half a step. It's progress. I decapitate three yagi before Ion intercedes.

"Ilsa, come with me," he says, blocking my sword strokes with his blades.

I try to push his blades away, but he's too strong for me. I lift my swords higher and try to twist, to swing, block, something, but this is beyond my skill level, and even as he forces my movement to a standstill, the wailing yagi freeze my frame.

And Ion knows it. He does some sort of fancy flicking thing with his sword, and disarms my right hand, flinging the blade away into the yagi-filled darkness.

He clamps his hand around my other hand, the one still holding a sword. He angles the blade away from himself, almost behind me, as though to stab Ram if he gets too close.

I'm panting, knackered already. And, yeah, also completely terrified. Focusing all my strength on moving one body part against the paralyzing sound waves, I slip my empty hand to my hip and wrap my fingers around the hilt of my saber, unsure of my next move, or if I'll even be able to move. Ram has his hands full with yagi and I still haven't seen Ozzie. I hope she's okay. If the yagi got to her again...

"Come with me, Ilsa. You can be human."

"What good would I be to you human?" Unless I completely misunderstood his earlier implications, Ion wants me to bear his dragon babies — something I might have actually considered if he hadn't proven himself to be a narcissistic bugger who wants to kill me.

Ion laughs. "More use than dead."

As he's speaking, one of the yagi lunges toward me, horns down to skewer me, and with a jolt of terror that's enough to free my hand from its frozen state, I pull the saber from my hip, catching the yagi under the chin (not that they really have chins), and slicing its head half off its body before kicking the carcass over.

Ion still has my left hand tight in his, and now he lunges to grab my right hand as well, but instead of pulling my hand away, I whip the saber around toward him. Movement begets movement—it seems to be the key to overcoming the paralyzing wails. My sword sings as it whips through the air.

This is the move that sliced so many round steaks this summer, that freed so many flank steaks from the loin. And it very nearly severs Ion's ribs, too.

He releases my hand and leaps back as the tip of the saber grazes his shirt.

I'd love to feel triumphant at this moment, and it's great to have the use of my left hand again, but the look on Ion's face erases any thrill of victory I might feel.

He is no longer trying to woo me, or even toying with thoughts of letting me live. Cold fury radiates from his face, through his body, and down his blade as he swings it toward me.

I leap out of the way just in time, half stumbling over a yagi twitching on the ground. There are two more yagi behind me and I swing my blades butterfly style, never mind that one sword is a saber. Their heads roll and I step past them, kicking their bodies toward Ion.

He leaps over them, through the air toward me,

sword raised. I'm still drawing back from kicking the yagi. He's faster and his blade is coming down toward me. I lean back but his sword is long, far longer than the distance I can lean.

But at the same moment, I hear a snapping growl behind me and Ozzie leaps over my head, into Ion, into his blade.

I stumble away over fallen yagi, decapitate two more, spin around to see what's become of Ion. He's only got one sword now, as far as I can see.

Another yagi lunges toward me. I sever its head, my attention mostly on Ion and Ram and Ozzie.

What happened to Ozzie? The ground is a mass of twitching yagi in the darkness, and I don't dare look any closer. Ion bounds toward me and I whip my saber back as I dart behind a tree.

Ion swings his sword.

I duck behind the tree.

He sidesteps the tree and swings again.

I dive behind another tree, but we're getting closer to the lake, and trees are fewer here. Soon I won't have anywhere left to hide.

Ion's hungry grin says he knows it, too.

I scramble backward, unwilling to turn my back on Ion, though I can't move as quickly as he can when he can see where he's going and I have no idea what I might bump into behind me. The unearthly wail of yagi has died down, at least. I think we've killed most of them.

Ion sidesteps another tree. He swings his sword at my neck. I sprint for the lake, splashing into the shallows in my stocking feet. Ion follows me, laughing, swelling, growing.

He's going to turn into a dragon, isn't he?

Ram charges toward us, breathing fire at Ion as I wade deeper into the lake to escape the flames. As I watch, Ram leaps forward, morphing into a dragon as he lunges through the air, still breathing fire, extending his talons toward Ion as though to shred him on impact.

But just as quickly, Ion changes, too. Talons meet talons with the sound of a score of swordsmen, blade on blade, piercing the night as fire billows from their mouths.

I'm rib-deep in the lake now and duck to avoid the flames. When I come up for air a moment later, the two dragons are in the sky, screaming and clashing and tearing at one another. Ram slashes at Ion, who brings his spiked tail around like a club to block the blow. But just as quickly, Ram pivots in the air, coming up under Ion headfirst, aiming the two pointed horns on his head at Ion's belly.

Ion doesn't have time to move out of the way.

Ram's horns make contact and rip through Ion's underbelly.

Blood drips from the monster as Ion turns his back on Ram and flies away through the night, clutching his injuries with both hands.

Ram slashes after him only briefly before swooping around, lowering himself down from the sky with his mighty wings even as he returns to human form, his wings the last to go. He lands in the shallows facing me, wearing a pair of boxer shorts and his swords. He's panting.

I wade through the water toward him. "Where's Ozzie? Is she okay?" I'm about to step past him when he stretches his arm out, catches me, and pulls me against his shoulder.

I instinctively tense — this is too similar to the way Ion caught me, held me, and threatened me mere moments ago. But Ram's hold is not tight.

"Don't look." His words are heavy, almost choking.

The moonlight reflects off the water and I can see more clearly here than I have all night. I look into Ram's face. More than sweat is dripping down his face.

Is he crying?

I can see clearly that he is. I just can't quite accept that it's true. Ram doesn't strike me as the crying type. Invincible guys don't cry, do they?

"She wanted it this way. She wanted to go down fighting, not wasting away."

"No." I shake my head and stumble past Ram, splashing in the shallows. "No!"

I reach the campsite. The twitching yagi have nearly stilled, a vaporous mist rising from their bodies, stinging my eyes. I can see Ozzie's still form among them, completely motionless, Ion's sword jutting up through her chest.

I start to pick my way past the yagi toward her.

"There's nothing you can do for her. She's dead." Ram's hand falls on my shoulder.

Torn between struggling forward to Ozzie and turning away, I stop still, stare a moment longer, and then let Ram pull me backward, away from the fallen yagi and the stinging vapor that's rising from their dissipating bodies.

"No," I whisper, even though I know it's true, even though I know she's gone, there's nothing I can do, and she probably wasn't going to make it home, anyway. "She was protecting me. That sword was meant for me. I'm alive because — " grief chokes off my words and I can only point feebly toward the dog who was a friend to me when I had no other friends.

"She wanted it this way," Ram whispers.

I look him full in the face, wanting to protest, to insist that a guy who can transform into a dragon should have been able to save my dog, but I know that's not true. Theoretically, I can transform into a dragon, too, but that didn't help Ozzie.

So instead of saying anything I just stare at Ram that much longer, watching the tears overflow his eyes until I don't think I can stand any longer and I reach my hand toward him to steady myself.

Ram's hand is still on my shoulder. As I lean in toward him, he wraps his arm around me and settles my head against his chest. I can feel the grief choking inside him helplessly, and I bawl alongside him, ugly sobs that wrack my body with lurching spasms of hurt.

I'm crying harder than I ever cried into Ozzie's shoulder, and on top of loss I feel guilt, that Ozzie died to protect me, that Ram lost his dog because of me, that Ram gave me his dog and I got her killed.

On the tail of my guilt comes resentment that I am a hunted thing. I didn't ask to be a dragon. I don't *want* to be a dragon. For so long I wanted to know who I am, but now that I know, I almost wish I could un-know it. Or better yet, be something else.

But didn't Ion offer me that already?

Temptation and grief war inside me, fueled by guilt that somehow I did this, that if I was other than what I am, Ozzie would still be alive.

I place my hands against Ram's collarbones and peel my face away from his chest. I can see his eyes again. They're lovely, glowing like starlight, twinkling like sapphires. But Ion's eyes are lovely, too.

"Ion said they could make me human."

Ram freezes, his stare suddenly turned to ice.

"Just human," I continue. "Not a dragon anymore."

Ram shakes his head slowly. "No. It doesn't work like that."

"How do you know? Maybe it can. Ion said it can."

Ram narrows his eyes slightly—not angry, but just like he's trying to understand. "Is that what you really want?"

The answer is so obvious, I almost choke on it. "Ozzie is dead because I'm a dragon."

"Ozzie is dead because of Ion."

"Because I'm a dragon." I don't want to fight with him. "Ion understood. I didn't even have to tell him how I felt. He knew. He came to me and offered that they could make me human—only human."

Ram's jaw clenches so tight I can see it under his eyes, in spite of his beard. "Do you know how he knew?"

"Because he understands me."

"No. No." Ram draws a deep breath, shaking his head slowly, and once again, apology fills his eyes. I am so sick of seeing apology in his eyes. He sucks in another breath, kind of ragged this time, like he's fighting to tell me something he desperately doesn't want to say.

"What?" I prompt him.

"That's how your mother died."

Chapter Thirteen

"What?" I choke on the question.

"Eudora told your mother she could make her only human. After her victory making the yagi, people believed her. Your mother went to her. Until that moment, no one realized your mother was a dragon, or that there even was another female dragon besides Eudora."

"I thought your mother—"

"My mother had died by then."

"Oh. I'm sorry."

Ram dips his head in acknowledgement. His beard twitches and he finds his words. "Your mother's name was Faye. Faye Goodwin. She went to Eudora, but it was a trap. Faye realized it too late and tried to get away. But your father had someone working near Eudora, keeping an eye on her—"

"A spy?"

"Yes. Your father had a spy watching Eudora. He got word of what was happening and flew to your mother's rescue. That's how they met—when he arrived to free her. Unfortunately, she was gravely injured by this time. He took her as far as he could and tried to nurse her back to health. In the process they fell in love.

"The yagi tracked them down and attacked. Your father tried to defend her, but Eudora fought him. The yagi killed your mother."

It's a long time before either of us speak. Somehow, even though I've always known my mother was dead, hearing how she died makes it more real. And terrible.

"Didn't you say before that you were there — that you helped my father escape?"

Ram hangs his head as though ashamed. "I did what I could. Your mother was badly injured already, and we were vastly outnumbered. To be honest, my biggest concern was getting the egg to safety without anyone knowing it ever existed, before the yagi destroyed it, too."

"The egg?"

"Your egg. You." Ram's eyes twinkle for the first time since he landed in the lake and saw I was okay.

"She died before I was born." I repeat the words I'd heard before but never understood.

"Technically, before you were hatched. Your father took the egg back to Azerbaijan and hid you in the village — we were, at least, successful in keeping the egg hidden, and keeping your existence a secret for several years. I don't know how or when Eudora learned about you. I'm sure she has spies. Ion is one of them."

I clench my eyes shut at this news. I don't want Ion to be a spy. I want to be able to trust him. Ion offered to make me human, and I really want that to be an honest, valid option.

But no amount of wanting can make it so. Ion killed Ozzie. He would have killed me.

Ram's words cut through my thoughts. "I don't want to rush you, but we should probably get going."

"Right." I suck in a shaky breath. I'm rather glad we have practical, tangible things to think about. Steps to take. Stuff to do, rather than wallow in grief and confusion. "What happened to your clothes?"

Ram looks down at his boxer shorts — a striped blue pair that look right fit on him, but don't tell anyone at

Saint Evangeline's I said so. He shrugs. "Clothes don't survive the switch. My swords stay on—even my backpack would have stayed on if I'd been wearing it—because my wings come out from my shoulders. They don't tear the straps away. But my chest and arms get too big for my shirt, and my legs get too big for my pants. The only reason my boxer shorts survive is because they have an elastic waist. To be honest, they don't always make it."

He's blushing slightly, and I laugh. I'm not sure why I'm laughing, I guess just because he looks embarrassed, which is a huge improvement over apologetic.

At the same time, I know enough of what he looks like as a dragon to imagine how the boxer shorts survived. Even though he grows enormously, his dragon waist is relatively tiny, like on a greyhound, a narrow band between his barrel chest and strong legs.

Also, I might be laughing because he's cute, and the thought of him as a dragon makes my stomach flutter in a way that's completely unfamiliar and somewhat unsettling.

Ram picks his way past the yagi corpses to our campsite, finds his backpack, and shuffles off a safe distance from their stinking vapor to put on more clothes. I, too find something dry to wear, and duck behind some bushes to change. When I step back around the bushes, Ram has removed Ozzie's body from among the yagi, and is using his cutlass to dig a hole a safe distance from their potentially-hallucinogenic stink.

I join him, and we dig in silence, stopping only to decide if the hole is deep enough yet. We unearth several large stones as we dig, and I set these aside. Once Ram has placed Ozzie in the hole and covered her with dirt, I put the stones on top to keep animals from disturbing her body. Ram pulls several more rocks from the lake, settling a large stone on its end near her head as a marker.

With the tip of his dagger, he carves letters into the rock.

Azi.

"Azi." I have to say the name out loud to make the connection. Ozzie is Azi. I've never seen it written before—I just assumed, when Ram told me the dog's name, that it was Ozzie.

"I named her after a friend who saved my life in the war."

"Which war?" I ask partly out of curiosity, partly to make polite conversation instead of this heavy silence, but I realize as soon as I've asked the question that I probably won't know the war, if it's a dragon skirmish or something out of Azeri history, which I know nothing about.

But Ram surprises me. "World War Two. My friend Azi was a soldier who saved my life. It's a good name, a heroic name."

Ram is staring at the name on the rock, lost in thought, and I'm frantically doing math.

World War Two ended almost fifty years ago.

If Ram fought in World War Two, he would have to be, like, seventy years old. Elderly.

I look him up and down. He's not elderly.

"World War Two?" I repeat incredulously. "Which World War Two?" All I can think is maybe the Azeris have their own accounting of the world wars. Maybe their World War Two happened more recently. Maybe that's how they refer to the breakup of the Soviet Union, or something. Yeah, that would make sense. Not a lot of sense, but a blooming bit more sense than the idea that Ram is elderly.

Maybe I breathed in too much of the yagi vapor after all.

Ram chuckles. "The only one." He tucks his dagger back into the scabbard on his thigh and looks around, as though checking to make sure we've got everything we need.

Faint light colors the eastern horizon. The sun will be rising soon.

"The one that ended in 1945?" I clarify.

"Yes." He's walking back toward the lake, circling the bank.

I hurry to keep up. "And what year is it now?" This may seem like a stupid question, but it's occurred to me that maybe this whole dragon-changing stuff might have plunged us into a completely different decade, or something. Far-fetched, yes, but what other explanation is there? And that wouldn't be the weirdest revelation he's made in the last few days.

"It's 1993."

"That's what I thought. So World War Two ended, what, forty-eight years ago?"

"Yes." Ram pauses. "When I was in the air, I saw another stream feeding into the lake from the east. It probably originates in the mountains. We should be able to follow it into the mountains, then find another stream on the other side to follow to the Danube."

"The Danube?" I repeat, not because I've never heard of the longest river in Europe, but because most of my intellectual faculties are still trying to harmonize Ram's age with the date of the war he claims to have fought in.

Ram explains, "The Danube swings sharply north from the Bulgarian border to the southern tip of Moldova. We won't be able to reach the Black Sea — or get you home — without crossing it. We can fly over it, of course, but for now we'll have to walk. Sun's coming up."

I nod, understanding the geography well enough, still focused on what he said about fighting in World War Two. But at the same time, something else has caught my attention. Steam is rising from the heap of dead yagi. And they're making a rustling sound, almost as though they're coming back to life. "What's up with the yagi?" I point to the nearest corpses just visible in the woods beyond us.

"They're diffusing." Ram must see the questions on my face, because he explains, "They're not stable. It's only the dark magic that makes them live at all. By the time they get to this stage most of the neurotoxin in their vapor has dissipated — unless they're in an enclosed room. Their insides evaporate quickly once they die, and their exoskeletons wither to nothing."

"To nothing?"

"Kind of like when you burn paper in a fireplace." He leads me past the pile in a wide circle, toward the stream he talked about following. "If it burns under the right conditions, you can still see the charred form of the paper, even read the print from the page, but if you touch it, it turns to dust. Same thing with the yagi. They've never been scientifically classified because no one has ever been able to study a dead one."

I can see the exoskeletons curling and shriveling as we move past the dead yagi. Interesting as Ram's explanation may be, it doesn't distract me from what we were talking about moments before—something I want to know more about, even if I'm a bit scared to hear the answer.

"How old are you?"

"I'm mature." Ram reaches the stream and begins to follow it.

"A number." I tromp along beside him. "*Mature* is not a number. For example, I'm eighteen."

"How old do I look?"

"Twenty-ish."

Ram nods. "Let's go with that, then."

"But you said you fought in World War Two?"

"I've fought in many wars. Not all of them have names."

He is obviously trying to evade my real question, which is irritating, and only makes me more determined to learn the real answer.

I deliberately over-enunciate. "What year were you born?"

Ram makes a face. "Dragons don't age like humans. We don't grow old and weak and die. Dragons live forever—unless they're killed. Do you know what year your father was born?"

I try to recall if I've ever heard anything that would give me a clue about my dad's age. He looks pretty young, for a dad. Dark hair. No gray that I've ever noticed. Nor have I ever spotted any wrinkles, though much of his face is hidden by his neatly-trimmed beard. I remember once when I was a little girl, somebody wishing my father a happy birthday, but he waved it off and said he'd had too many birthdays to bother celebrating anymore. At the time, I'd figured *too many birthdays* was thirty or forty.

Now I'm not so sure. "What year?"

"Let's see—was it 1784, or 1786? I can never quite remember."

"That's over two hundred years ago."

"He's still young. Your mother was older than your father, you know. She was born in the sixteen hundreds, I don't know exactly when. I don't even know if she knew."

"But she was still young enough to…lay an egg?"

"Female dragons lay one or more eggs every year or so until they're about six or seven hundred years old."

"Seriously?"

Ram shrugs, still walking at a fairly brisk pace, but not so fast I can't keep up. "That's what I've been told, at least. I haven't known any egg-laying females personally. But I've heard Eudora is past egg-laying age."

"What year were you born?" I'm not going to lie, my pulse is kind of pounding by this point. I'm not even sure why—I guess just because the things we're talking about are so beyond my experience, and yet so intricately bound to me.

"I was born in 1925." Ram is picking a path for us along the grassy bank. The trees grow tight to the stream, and Ram takes my hand so I can walk just behind him, and we help each other keep our balance.

"So you're sixty-eight years old?"

"Sixty-seven. My birthday's in November. But I'm not sixty-seven like you think of sixty-seven year-olds. Think of it this way: Azi was twelve. In human years, she'd be a pre-teen. In dog years, that makes her eighty-four. She was very, very old for a dog of her size, but compared to a human being, she was just a kid."

"So, what then? You're saying in human years you're

fifteen or something? What does that make me? Three?" I'm not actually doing math, here, in case you're wondering. I'm just trying to play it cool like my heart isn't slamming inside my ribcage for reasons I don't understand. I don't even know why I care how old Ram is, or how our ages match up. But judging by the way my blood is screaming through my veins, it's important to me.

"I'm an adult. You're an adult."

"I'm an adult?" I have to stop walking. I about didn't get all those words out, even though there were only three of them. My face is probably red. I try to bluff past it. "Why have I never laid an egg, then?"

"You can only lay an egg as a dragon. And the egg won't develop unless you..." Ram coughs, inexplicably tongue-tied. "Have a mate." He's stopped walking, too, and dropped my hand. Now he crouches down by the stream. "Why don't we get a drink? I'm thirsty."

"Great idea."

The stream is cold, the water refreshing. I scoop it up by handfuls, my thoughts mostly consumed with everything Ram has told me. From the way he tells it, I could live a very long time. My dad is crazy old. My mom—well, now I know why I never found her picture at Saint Evangeline's. If she attended when she was my age, photographs hadn't been invented yet. And I wasn't looking nearly far enough back in the yearbooks.

My thirst quenched, I stand and stretch, yawning. "I didn't get much sleep last night."

"We've had a couple nights like that now." He turns and faces me.

Part of me wishes he'd turn back around, so I wouldn't have to face him as we talk. His eyes are so blue, so piercing, as though they can see right through me to the jumbled thoughts inside.

But part of me is also curious to look at him, to think about how long he's been around and how much longer he'll live, and wonder what he'd look like without the beard.

Ram balances his hands on the hilts of the swords at his hips. "I don't know how much longer we should go on like this."

"Like what?" My face feels warm, and I wonder if he can read my thoughts after all.

"Walking. It could take us months to get you home at this rate, and we'd have to go around the Black Sea."

"What's the other option? Fly over it?"

Ram nods. "I can teach you to fly, a little bit tonight, a little further tomorrow night, so by the time we reach the sea, you'll be able to fly across."

"It's a big sea."

"It is. I don't think you could make it on your first flight. Changing into a dragon is enormously draining, especially when you're not used to it."

He'd said something like that before, so I'm not surprised. At the same time, though, I feel slightly panicked. I don't want to change into a dragon. I don't want to *be* a dragon. In fact, I'm pretty sure I don't even want dragons to exist, except that my father and Ram are both dragons, and they're two of my favorite people in the world.

This is tricky.

"So, what are you saying?" I ask, kicking myself when my voice trembles, betraying my fear.

Ram's expression is kind. Maybe even understanding, though I doubt he really gets where I'm coming from.

He's changed into a dragon flawlessly before my eyes. And he seems perfectly cool with his reptilian alter-ego. "I think we should eat a big meal to help build your strength up, then rest for a while so you can try flying tonight."

I nod silently, not trusting my voice. Food sounds good. Rest would be welcome. But the dragon-changing thing? I'm not ready.

So.

Not.

Ready.

Still, that's not until tonight. And as the last couple days have proven, anything could happen before tonight.

Chapter Fourteen

The weird thing about making camp is that it's just the two of us now. No Azi, no Ion. And I'm not used to falling asleep in the daylight, never mind that I'm exhausted and singlehandedly ate a roast goose (Ram caught one for each of us). So we stretch out on our leaf beds in the shade, with our heads sort of together and our feet on opposite sides of a clump of flowers, like a triangle missing its side because I can't quite bring myself to lie down alongside this guy (is that weird? I just can't).

I ask Ram about the dragon-changing thing. "How do you change into a dragon, anyway? Do you just blow yourself up like a balloon?" I saw more of Ion than Ram, and Ion did that laughing bit like he was sucking in air.

Ram props himself on his side with his elbow on the ground and his hand under his ear. He's facing me, but I'm on my back staring up into the leafy canopy above us. Ram explains, "For me, it's like I'm holding my breath, but not really holding my breath. You have to visualize yourself changing, but most importantly, you have to *want* to change. Otherwise you could accidentally pop into dragon form when you sneeze. That could be a problem."

His words are light and I suspect he's trying to make me laugh, but I pinch my eyes shut in despair.

You have to *want* to change?

"Ilsa? You falling asleep already?"

"No." I could try faking it, but Ram knows me too well for that. "What if I can't do it?"

"It's going to take a lot longer to get you home, then."

He inhales slowly. "I started changing when I was a kid. Most dragons do. For your safety, though, your father thought it best that you wait until you're older."

"Is there such a thing as waiting too long?" My voice has grown thick, but I can't help it.

"I don't know. I've known so few dragons, and all of them have been dragons for as long as I've known them." He falls onto his back and looks up into the leaves, too. "I hope not."

*

By evening we've slept and eaten again, and Ram is ready to teach me how to become a dragon. He faces me in the middle of a field, looks me full in the face, and frowns.

"You look terrified."

I don't respond to the accusation with more than a shrug.

"Don't be frightened. You don't even have to fly the first time, if you don't want to—but flying is the best part. And just think how quickly you'll be able to get home. I thought you wanted to get home."

"I wanted nothing more than to get home," I acknowledge. "But that was when I thought..."

"Thought what?"

"That home would be the same place I left as a child. That I'd fit in there."

"You *will* fit in."

"I don't know anything about it. And I'm the only dragon."

"You say *dragon* like it's a bad word."

I told you he could read me too well. "Ion is a dragon. He's bad. Eudora is a dragon."

"Your father is a dragon. So was your mother. I'm a

dragon. The dragons I know are some of the wisest, most benevolent creatures, fiercely protective of their people—"

"It's that fiercely protective part that worries me. Dragons are capable of such violence." I shudder.

"*Capable of* is different from *prone to*." Ram makes a commiserating face. "Look at it this way—if you become a dragon, you'll be one of the good ones. You can choose. You define who you are and how you act. I can't imagine you being bad."

Protests rise in my mind—of the looks the girls at Saint Evangeline's gave me when they caught me eating chicken bones, of all the ways I never fit in, of the fact that I don't want to be a dragon. Isn't that bad?

But the way Ram looks at me, like he believes in me, I almost want to live up to his version of me. And I'm rather certain he'd understand about the chicken bone thing. You should have seen him tear into that roast goose.

So I take his hands, which he's been holding out toward me for a bit, and I grit my teeth. "Okay. Let's do this."

Ram holds my hands securely and leans his head down toward mine.

I duck away. "Whoa, what are you doing?"

"This is how my father taught me how to change."

"How?"

"He held my hands, and pressed his forehead to mine, and I changed as he changed."

"So we're just going to pinch our eyes shut and say the magic words?"

"There are no magic words. Picture yourself as a dragon. Feel the change—your nails extending into talons, your wings arching out from your back, your skin tightening, buckling into scales…" Ram's voice drifts off.

I'm trying to feel the changes he describes, trying to imagine myself becoming that thing like I watched Ion become. The next thing I know, Ram is a dragon.

I look down at myself with a surge of terrified excitement—

And I'm still human.

Ram switches back. He's still in his boxer shorts, which he stripped down to in preparation for changing, because he's already destroyed enough clothes on this trip, and if I don't hurry up and figure out how to become a dragon and fly home, he's going to run out of clothing. Not that I'd complain. Personally, I think he looks mighty fine in his boxer shorts—crazy beard notwithstanding.

"Are you sure I'm a dragon?" I ask when he gives me a look that questions what went wrong. "Maybe I was switched at birth. Maybe it skips a generation. Maybe I'm a dud."

"Maybe you don't want to be a dragon." He crosses his arms over his chest.

I cross my arms, too, and meet his eyes, but I have no snarky comebacks.

"All right, Ilsa." He spreads his arms wide in a gesture of defeat. "You tell me. How can I make you want it?"

I have to bite my lip and turn my head away. Did I mention that Ram is not wearing a shirt, and he looks very good not wearing a shirt? I did mention that, didn't I? Yeah, probably because I can't stop thinking about that.

"You know you're going to have to walk home if you

can't fly, don't you?"

"Actually, I've been thinking about that."

"And?"

"You said you could fly and carry Azi home, right? Why can't you carry me? I weigh less than Azi." Technically, I'm not sure that's true about my weight. The girls at school were always horrified when they saw how much I weigh. I'm not fat—not at all. I'm just a very dense person. I always figured it's because muscle weighs more than fat, and I took it as a good indicator that I was stronger than all the waif-girls at school.

After all, I did a lot of strength-training activities. I was on the rowing team and I did archery. The archery was especially fun because every year we'd go up to Scotland to the Highland Games and do exhibition shoots with things like moving targets and flaming arrows. It was one of my favorite parts of school.

I probably would have done fencing, too, if I'd have known it would end up being so important, but the fencing time conflicted with rowing practice and I didn't want to let my team down. They needed me. Most of the other girls were waifs.

"You didn't like it when Ion carried you," Ram reminds me, but his expression says he's thinking about it.

"That's because he was trying to kidnap me. And he was holding me rather tight."

"You can ride on my back, actually," Ram concedes, though he looks disappointed. "Don't you at least want to give it another try?"

For his sake I try again, but my heart is not in it. I mostly just want him to carry me.

So when he turns into a dragon and I don't, he kneels

down low in front of me and I climb onto his back, between his wings. He still has his backpack on, the straps looped around the joints where his wings sprouted from his shoulders, and he's wearing his swords, just as I'm wearing mine.

I lean close against his back, loop my arms up under his wings, and hold on as well as I can without hurting him. Unlike some pictures I've seen of dragons, Ram doesn't have spiny plates coming out of his back like a stegosaurus. I can only assume those artists got dragons confused with dinosaurs.

But in a lot of other ways, Ram looks like the classic artistic depictions of a dragon, including horns and a long scaled tail. But unlike some pictures, which show a tail with an arrow-head-like tip, Ram's tail has four spikes jutting out sideways...much like a stegosaurus. So I totally understand how artists could get the two confused. Unlike the horns on his head, which are pointy-sharp on the tips, Ram's tail spikes are rather blunted, more of a smashing weapon than the slicing spears that protrude from his skull.

He beats his wings and we rise above the treetops, gliding eastward. His movements are smooth, strong, graceful. As he picks up speed I wrap my arms more securely around his neck, careful not to squeeze him. Flying is a bit frightening, but mostly exhilarating.

Ram is careful to avoid towns and highways, or anywhere people might be. The night is cloudy, though, so I doubt we could be seen. He's not even glowing much. He's just slightly iridescent tonight. I wonder if he has an internal dimmer switch to control how brightly he glows.

At first it's a tad terrifying being up so high,

especially since my last experience in the air was when Ion hurled me toward the earth. But before long I relax and try to see what I can of the land and where we're headed.

There are mountains ahead of us — they look like jutting shadows in the night, but I recall from Ion's road atlas that the Carpathian Mountain Range dominates the Romanian landscape, and Ram had said the stream we were following probably originated there.

We fly on and on, it's difficult to say how long. Hours? I'm watching the mountains grow larger as we get closer, but at the same time, dark shapes loom above the mountaintops, and lights flicker ominously.

A thunderstorm is building beyond the mountains. As we draw closer, I realize the storm is moving toward us, swelling as it approaches. Soon I can hear the thunder, and see streaks of lightning instead of mere flickering lights.

We haven't been flying that long. I doubt it's even midnight yet, but I don't think we'll be able to go much farther. The storm looks dangerous.

Like the stillness before the storm, the air around us is stagnant and heavy with humidity. Ram begins to sag in the sky. We had a bit of a breeze when he started out, and I think the air currents helped him stay aloft and glide. Ram has been beating his wings hard to stay above the trees, but soon the leaves seem to reach up as though to grab us, and the thunder threatens, growing louder and more fearsome the further we fly.

Just as I'm beginning to worry that Ram is going to scrape the treetops, he swerves toward a building in the distance.

I've seen several of these from the air, mostly in

remote areas, their architecture varying from medieval to gothic, baroque to neoclassical, from classic castles with enclosed courtyards to sprawling country villas, all of them in varying states of disrepair. Most looked abandoned, as does this one. But it is night and looks can be deceiving.

Ram swoops toward the fortress, over its high crumbling walls, and sets down gently in the courtyard. I slide off his back and land on my feet as he converts to human form.

He's still wearing his boxer shorts. Yes, I checked.

But he's also panting heavily, doubled over, gripping his knees, maybe even trembling.

"Are you okay? What's wrong?"

"I'm fine." He doesn't sound fine. He sounds knackered.

Horrified, I realize what's wrong. "I'm too heavy for you, aren't I?"

Ram shakes his head. "It's not you. I'm not used to carrying someone when I fly. I've fought Ion and the yagi, hiked through the woods, changed for you, changed again—"

"Changing takes a great deal of energy," I recall aloud, trying to keep my voice down in case this place, which looks abandoned, isn't.

"I just need a breather. When the wind died down, I lost the updrafts and had to beat my wings more. It's all part of the equation."

"Can I do anything for you? Can I get you something to eat?" I look around. There are doorways on all sides of the courtyard, hidden under the shadows of a second-story walkway perched atop arched supports. Some of the doors are closed, some open. Some doors appear to be missing altogether. I peer toward them and they gape back, toothless voids that could hide anything.

I shiver. The night is cold and the storm is drawing closer, bringing frigid mountain air. Lightning crackles through the sky, illuminating the courtyard like a strobe light. I don't know where we're going to find any food.

Ram hasn't answered my question. He's pulled his backpack off and is stepping into a pair of jeans.

"Where are we?"

"I'm not sure exactly." He tugs a t-shirt on over his head and slips his arms into the sleeves of a flannel shirt. "The Romanian government—really most governments of Eastern Europe—seized control of royal estates following the World Wars. They claimed they were taking them for the public good, but in most cases, they failed to keep the buildings in proper repair. Now that the Iron Curtain has fallen, governments are trying to return the estates to the families who originally owned them, but the process is lengthy. A lot of these places are still abandoned."

"Is this particular place abandoned?" Lightning flickers again, and I can hear rain approaching. We step toward the shelter of the second-floor balcony, ducking cautiously through an archway, unsure what we'll find.

"It looks abandoned, but I don't know. It could be the family has only recently claimed it. They might be living in part of the building while they slowly rebuild the rest." Rain starts to patter above us as Ram speaks.

"So somebody could be here?"

Lightning flashes again, and I instinctively step closer to Ram. He's still adjusting his swords over his shirt, but once he has the holster buckle tight, he leans toward me. "It's possible. But if they're asleep for the night, it shouldn't be a problem. We only need to rest awhile and get out of the rain."

"Where do you want to rest?" I peer toward the nearest doorway as lightning flashes, illuminating the room. The space looks empty, the door leaning inward on one hinge.

"Anywhere. Just not in the courtyard. Ion may still be looking for us."

I nod, though it doesn't seem likely to me that Ion would be out in this storm. Then again, Ram glows faintly when he's a dragon. If Ion was anywhere in the area, he may have seen Ram flying overhead and noted where he went down.

Ion might even guess that Ram would be exhausted.

Ram steps ahead of me into the room. The far wall has three windows, only one of which has any glass at all, and that just a single pane. The wind, which has picked up considerably now that the storm has hit, spits rain in sideways onto the stone floor.

Broken glass litters the far end of the room. Otherwise, there is little else here. A wooden chair, and a large cabinet that fills one side wall.

Ram approaches the cabinet cautiously.

"What do you think it is? A wardrobe?"

"Or a door to the next room. I'm just checking to make sure we're alone." He has one hand on a sword hilt as he reaches for the handle.

I grip my swords as well, just to be safe.

I'm not sure if Ram timed it purposely, but he tugs the door open just as a large flash of lightning shocks the darkness into white light, and screams erupt throughout the room.

Chapter Fifteen

I duck toward the floor as the screaming bats circle chaotically overhead. The room is dark now, so I have no idea how many were in the closet. Plenty.

"Well." Ram's voice is close to my ear, and I realize he's hovering just above me, covering me, protecting me from the onslaught of flying mammals. "If anyone *is* home, we'll probably meet them soon. I can't imagine anyone could sleep through that."

A rumble of thunder nearly buries his words.

"Are they gone?"

"The bats? I don't know if they left the room, but they're not flying around so much. It may be safe to leave now, but stay low."

I run, crouching, my arms over my head to keep the critters from flying into my hair. Ram stays over me until we're back in the courtyard, under the protection of the walkway above, peering into the sheets of rain that make it impossible to see across the square.

I shudder. "Bats are so creepy."

"They eat bugs. They're useful." It almost sounds like Ram's defending them.

"We're not related to them, are we?"

He laughs. "Hardly. They're flying mammals that turn into vampires. We're humans who turn into flying reptiles. Two totally different species."

I can't tell if he's joking or not. The way he talks, in his usual serious voice, it's almost as though he believes vampires are real. "Do you think any of those bats are going to turn into vampires?"

"Did their eyes glow red?"

"I don't think so." Not that I was really looking.

"Most bats are just bats—just like most humans are just humans, and most lizards are just lizards. Although Romania has long been rumored to house the greatest remnant of the vampire population. Dracula's castle is not far from here."

"So, all the vampires should be there, not here, right?"

"Something like that, I'm sure," Ram says with a wink which I suppose is meant to indicate there's nothing to worry about. "Let's try the next room."

The door is closed, and I brace myself as he places one hand on the knob, but nothing flies out when he opens it.

This room has only one window, which appears to be mostly intact—a couple of the panes are cracked, but judging by the way the rain hits them, they're all still in place, at least. Leaves wave frantically in the wind on the other side of the glass. A bush or tree must have protected the window from the elements.

An upright piano occupies one wall, its keys dusty and warped with age. Next to it, a four-drawer filing cabinet stands sentinel in the corner, one drawer pulled out as though someone was looking for something before being suddenly called away. A settee with curved wooden legs sits near the opposite wall. Lightning flashes reveal its upholstery is faded but otherwise undamaged.

"This room is better preserved," Ram muses aloud.

"Yeah," I agree. "But why? Do you think somebody has been living here?"

He glances at the piano keys as lightning flickers again. The dust is thick and even. No one has touched the instrument in years, possibly decades.

"Think the sofa will hold us?" Ram steps toward the settee.

"It's probably full of mice, or worse," I predict, given our experience in the previous room.

Ram pulls out his saber and slaps the cushions with the flat side of the blade.

Dust billows into the air, and I duck my head behind his shoulder.

Ram slaps the cloud away. "I didn't hear any mice. Care to join me?"

"You first." I hold back for two reasons. One, I know Ram is exhausted and needs to get off his feet. And two, I really don't trust the couch. Not that it isn't still sturdy — judging from the palatial proportions of the abandoned estate, the couch and all the rest of the furnishings were probably top of the line, the best money could buy. And time hasn't been so hard on this room.

But sitting means putting my guard down, if only slightly. I'm not ready to do that yet. Ion or the yagi could show up any time.

Ram settles into the seat. It creaks a little, but that's all.

"Ah." He puts his feet up on the marble-topped occasional table in front of the settee.

Lightning sizzles through the sky, followed immediately by a sharp crack of thunder. The girls at Saint Evangeline's used to make a game of counting off the seconds between lightning and thunder to determine how close we were to the center of the storm.

I don't have to count anything to know we're close. Another flash, this one exceptionally bright, lights the room, sending shadows stretching across the floor and up the walls from the slender tree branches outside.

"Think it can hold both of us?" I step toward Ram.

"Join me." He pats the seat and I lower myself down, supporting some of my weight with my feet until I'm sure the aged sofa isn't going to give way. By the time I'm brave enough to settle my feet on the low table next to Ram's, his breathing is low and even. He's asleep.

It takes me several long minutes before I can relax, and it's not just because of the thunder and lightning. We left the door to the room standing partway open. We're slightly hidden behind it, since it opens to the side of the room with the piano and file cabinet, but being hidden also means being unable to see if someone steps through the doorway until they're a few steps into the room.

This doesn't reassure me.

That, and the way the lightning illuminates the flailing tree branches outside the window, sending their shadows thrashing across the walls and floor, I keep thinking I see movement. Or hands. Or faces.

It's probably nothing. Unless this place isn't abandoned. For all I know, those bats could be changing into vampires this very minute. Or, more likely but less encouraging, Ion and the yagi may have watched us fly through the night and followed us here. If that's the case, they could attack now, or keep following us until they feel they've found the perfect moment to strike.

*

Sunlight filters through the leaves outside the window, splashing across the stone floor, leaving slender rainbow prisms where the light passes through the cracks in the glass. I can only see it with one eye, the other being smashed against the shoulder of Ram's flannel shirt. His chest is rising and falling with even rhythm.

He must have been exhausted.

It's my fault, too, for making him fly with me on his back—for making him go on this blooming trip and fight Ion and the yagi all the time, to boot. I wouldn't feel so guilty about it, except that I know there's only one thing keeping us from flying straight home to my father—and that's the fact that I can't change into a dragon.

Yes, being a dragon is scary. No, I'm not yet used to the idea, or fond of it, or any of those things. But that doesn't matter. I *need* to turn into a dragon if we're going to make it home.

I'm also thirsty, if reluctant to leave Ram's side. It's a comfort being close to him. Reassuring, even. He's strong and gentle and I feel safe here. But I'm also crazy thirsty.

Carefully, I ease myself from the settee, hoping to slip away quietly without waking Ram.

His blue eyes open. "What time is it?"

"I've no idea. I don't even know what time zone we're in."

"The sun's been up awhile." Ram rises and steps toward the window.

"I suppose it has—not that it makes much difference. We ought to rest by day and fly at night, if the weather would cooperate." I walk toward the door. "Do you suppose the well in the courtyard has water in it?"

"Most likely." Ram looks out the window, then follows me to the courtyard, where, indeed, the well has water not more than ten feet down. The metal bucket is dented with age and the rope faded, but otherwise they appear to be in working order.

"I'm not going to fill it too full," I explain as I lower the bucket with the rope. "I'm not confident the rope can handle the weight of it full, and I don't want to lose the bucket."

"Good idea." Ram doesn't stand by to see how it goes. Instead he's circling the courtyard by the light of day. He travels all the way around before joining me at the well and pointing past me to a high archway. "The main door's nailed shut. Heavy beams, nails rusted through. It won't pop open easily."

I've drunk my fill and hand the bucket to Ram. "Suppose there's another door?"

He drinks the last of the water and lowers the bucket for more. "That, or maybe we can go through a window."

We check all the rooms methodically, looking out the windows. Halfway through, it becomes apparent we're not going to find a way out through the windows. The castle is surrounded by an old moat, emptied by time. We could go out a window, but it would be a twenty foot drop—or more, and then a sheer climb up the other side of the dry moat.

The leaves I saw outside the window of the room we slept in are the tippy-top branches of a straggly tree that sprouted from the bottom of the moat. But it's far too spindly to hold us, so there's no way we could climb out onto its branches to find our way down—not on that tree or any other.

We're stuck.

"Maybe you can breathe fire on the boarded-over door?" I suggest hopefully.

"By the time I burn through those beams, I'll likely have burnt away the bridge as well—not to mention the risk of burning the whole place down."

"It's too nice a place to risk that. Somebody ought to fix it up someday."

"I suppose they hope to, if they bothered to board

over the door to protect the inside from vandals. I'll have to fly us out of here."

"*We* can fly out of here." I amend his plans slightly. "I want to try again."

"Turning into a dragon?" Ram seems unsure of what I'm talking about, which strikes me odd, because what else would I be talking about?

"Of course. Don't you think I can?"

"Can? Theoretically, physiologically, yes, I think you can. But Ilsa." He turns to face me, and again I'm blown away by how blue his eyes are. "You have to *want* to change into a dragon. You didn't even come close last night, and I'm sure there's a reason for it."

"Well, I want to now." I do my best to look confident.

"Why?"

"Why what?"

"Why do you want to be a dragon?"

The day is growing warm as Ram is being daft. "So we can fly out of here."

Ram nods. "But why do you want to *be* a dragon?"

"I don't bloody well want to be a dragon," I snap impatiently. "I just want out of here."

"I'll fly you out." Ram looks only vaguely disappointed by my outburst. It seems more as though I've simply confirmed what he was trying to say the whole time.

"Look, no." I grab his arm. "I want to fly out of here as a dragon. You're tired. You shouldn't have to carry me."

"I'm well enough rested now. Besides, I won't stay a dragon long. We don't dare fly far, not in bright daylight when anyone could see us."

"We're in a remote part of the foothills, but whatever.

I'm just saying—let me try." I meet his eyes with my most imploring look.

"I don't mind letting you try." His expression is mostly patient, but something in his eyes snaps with intensity. "But I think you first need to examine why it is you don't really want to change. Until you address that, nothing's going to happen—"

I open my mouth to interrupt, but Ram raises his hand and continues his speech.

"And you're only going to make it worse. By trying and failing, you're only going to teach yourself how *not* to do it."

I wince slightly, not because I'm in pain, but because his words hit so close to something tender inside of me, but I don't know what it is. I draw in slow breaths while I study his eyes, still trying to come to terms with who this person is who's done so much for me.

Remember how I said, way back in Prague, that I don't really know him? That's changed somewhat. In some ways, I know him really well. I know he would fight his way through scores of yagi to keep me safe. I know I trust him more than I trust Ion—but why is that? In so many ways they're the same. Both dragons. Both of them are fighting over me, like I'm the ball in a game of keep-away, or the rope in a tug-o-war.

Why are they fighting over me, anyway? Because I'm female? Because Eudora sent Ion to kidnap me, and my dad hired Ram to bring me home?

Ram is just a guy my dad hired. He protects me because he's paid to. I tell myself that, but I'm not sure if I believe it. He has made greater sacrifices on my behalf than I feel I deserve. Exhaustion, hunger, the loss of his dog. Maybe all dragons are devoted like that.

It's his dragonishness that's so strange. The fact that he can fly, breathe fire, change into a reptile in a breath. The fact that he's sixty-seven years old, but not old, all at the same time.

Ram slips his hands into mine, watches me patiently as I wrestle with my thoughts.

I look him full in the face. "Can I try?"

"Do you want to be a dragon?"

I want to say 'yes,' but I can't lie to him. "I *want* to want to."

"It's not a means to an end. It's a thing in itself."

I grip his hands tighter. "Tell me why I should want to. Help me want it."

Ram dips his head closer to mine. Droplets of well water twinkle on his beard, glinting in the morning sun as he speaks. "A once-glorious race has been hunted nearly to extinction. If they're going to survive another generation, they need you."

His words are too reminiscent of what Ion said to me at the lake. Ion's statements have been bothering me for many reasons—not just because of what I understand them to mean, but also for what I don't.

"Hey Ram?"

"Yes?"

"About that—the next generation. Ion said—" I bite my lip, trying to think of what Ion said, exactly. He talked more with his hands than his words, his actions suggesting more than what he merely said.

"What?" Ram looks genuinely concerned.

Determined to accurately convey what passed between us, I replay the conversation in my mind, and shudder.

"What was it?" Ram's tone is tentative, as though he's

afraid I might be hurt, and doesn't want to make the hurt worse.

Or maybe I'm projecting that because of the weird confused pain I feel just thinking about what Ion said. "He said that he and I—" I shake my head. "I don't know, maybe I didn't hear him correctly, because he also said they could make me human, but I thought he was talking about dragons when he said…what he said."

"What did he say?"

"He said, 'you and I could be the start of a new generation.'"

Cold blue flashes in Ram's eyes and he looks up, into the sky. For an instant I'm sure he's going to change into a dragon that moment and fly off in a streak, chase down Ion and destroy him. And maybe I think that because his instinct is to do that very thing.

Chapter Sixteen

Ram doesn't move.

I'm a little scared to ask, but since we're on the subject, I do. "What do you think he meant by that?"

"I told you, you're the only female I know of who's of age to lay eggs."

"But he said they could make me human."

"He'll say whatever he thinks you want to hear. That doesn't make it true."

"So, you think he—"

"I think he had every intention of carrying you off and keeping you prisoner, raising a new generation of dragons with you."

"But you said Eudora wants to eliminate dragons from the earth, and Ion works for Eudora."

"They want power, more than anything. Domination. Eudora always claimed the best weapon against dragons is another dragon. They could raise your children to be mercenaries, like the yagi, only stronger, more invincible."

Ram's words peel back a curtain, and I stare down a dark hallway of ugly possibilities built on half-truths and lies. Maybe Ion wants to raise dragon-killing dragons with me. Maybe Ion's intentions are slightly more upright, but Eudora has been lying to him, luring him along with promises of children, when she really intends to work her mad scientist dark magic on his babies, and raise them to destroy their own kind.

"My children." I pull my hands from Ram's and take a step back, hugging myself. I've never put much thought into my own children, other than promising myself that I wouldn't ship them off to Saint Evangeline's, not without very good reason. (Not that I blame my father, so much. I know he was only protecting me, but it was awful, just the same.)

Ram lets me step away, but he is still close, within arm's reach. "Because of who you are, your children are vitally important. The identity of their father will be equally important."

I blow out a slow breath, and shake my head. "I didn't ask for any of this."

He stands there patiently awhile before he speaks. "You're not ready to change into a dragon yet, are you?"

I look at him. The words on the tip of my tongue are, 'are you crazy?' but I don't speak them, because I was the one begging him to let me try to change. Instead I say, "You know this isn't helping."

"I'm only telling you the truth of the situation." Ram raises his hands in an innocent gesture. "I'm not going to lie to you in order to get my way, or to make things easier for myself. I'm not Ion."

Even though he's being dead serious, I can't help smiling. I try to pinch the smile back, but that only makes my lips more determined to bend. "I'm glad you're not Ion."

Ram looks surprised and pleased. "I'm glad you're glad."

Bubbles of affection rise inside me. Ram is so patient. Sweet, even, if dragons can be sweet.

"Why don't I change and you climb on my back?" Ram asks. "We'll get out of here and get breakfast."

Yes, dragons can be sweet.

"Okay," I agree, and he does.

It's a very short flight. Up, over the walls, and down again into the wooded foothills not far from the castle. We don't dare go much further. Ram doesn't want to be seen—not by Ion or yagi or anyone else. I wrap my arms around his neck, not in a choke-hold, but more of a hug, and I press my face against his scales, which are surprisingly warm. Not sharp. Hard, but slightly pliant. Like dense leather, but of course shiny and slightly glowing.

And then we're standing in the woods, and Ram is a man again, digging through his backpack for pants and a shirt. From there it's the same old story, achingly familiar now. Ram hunts. We eat. We hike.

I mull my thoughts until they're too much for me, and then they spill over in hushed confession and a string of questions I don't expect Ram will even know how to answer. But I ask them, just the same.

"How do you know we deserve to survive?"

Ram doesn't seem surprised or offended. He just keeps walking beside me. We're climbing up the mountains now, the rocky streambed far wider than the actual stream. We're walking where the spring snowmelt travels, but it's fall now, so the path is clear and dry. "I guess I don't, not really." His words are tentative. He's sorting his thoughts as he talks. "What kind of egotist would presume to say they can choose who deserves to live and who should die? Eudora thinks she knows, and that's what makes her evil."

His judgment pinches something near my heart. I had been leaning toward the same side as Eudora—the idea that dragons don't belong in this world. But Ram makes a good point, one I need to think about more. Still, I have a backlog of questions to spill.

"We're dinosaurs, right? Shouldn't we have gone down with the T-rex?"

"Maybe. But we didn't, and I can't help but wonder if there's a reason *why*?"

"Why?" I echo.

"We're still here. We contribute something—something some folks think is important. Your villagers love you."

"What?" I can't think of anyone who's ever loved me besides my father. It's not a word I'm used to hearing. "They don't know me."

"You grew up there. You may not remember them, but they remember you and they long for your return. You're their princess, their protector, the keeper of the fire."

"Wait-wait-wait-wait." I don't know about this keeper of the fire bit or any of the other stuff, but the princess part strikes me as being particularly at odds with who I perceive myself to be. I mean, the girls at school were always making a big deal of their titles, and I always assumed I didn't have one. "Princess? You mean that figuratively, right?"

"You're the princess, the daughter of the Dragon King, Elmir."

"Is my dad a recognized government official?"

"He's recognized by his people. No one outside our region knows or cares what the people call your father. His is a position based not on power or politics, but on love."

And we're back to love again. I sigh.

Ram continues. He's really into this dragon heritage stuff. It seems like it's the one thing he feels comfortable talking about. "They love you, as they love your father, as they love fire and warmth and protection. They love you as they love their culture and heritage and ancestors, as they love the earth that feeds them and the clouds that shade them by day. Did you know a dragon's wings are fireproof?"

"Are they?" It makes sense, I guess, them breathing fire and all. His words remind me of the tiny introduction to Azerbaijan I read in Ion's road atlas. My land is a land of fire, shrouded in mystery. In the remote places, people live more like their ancestors did a thousand years ago than their peers elsewhere in the world today. Complete with dragon kings and everything, I guess.

"Legend says, when balls of fire fell from the sky and destroyed all other great lizards and all other life, the dragons wrapped their wings around their people and their children, but in doing so, they stretched them as far as they could go, and they could not cover themselves. They died in the rain of fire, but humanity was saved, along with the next generation of dragons — their dragon protectors. Those who pass through death together are knit together, their lives intertwined."

A tiny ache like homesickness wells up inside me, but I shake my head. "The dinosaurs died before there were any humans."

"Did they?"

Ram's question isn't a confident, challenging one, but two words spoken thoughtfully. They wriggle in between my doubts and take root there, like the tree that grew in the abandoned moat, stretching its leaves to the sun.

We hike longer in silence, topping a ridge among the mountains, catching a view of the majestic Romanian countryside, stopping again to eat and get off our feet.

"What do you think?" Ram asks as we feast on roast

pork from a wild boar he beheaded with a single stroke of his saber. "Shall we rest up and try flying again tonight? We'll cover more distance that way."

I had been happily devouring short ribs, but Ram's words act as a reminder I'm not ready to hear. Flying is a great idea—except for the part where I need to turn into a dragon. Ram may not mind carrying me, but I know it's hard on him, and I don't feel right about being a burden. Nonetheless, I can't think of a good reason not to accept his plan.

"That seems prudent," I acknowledge, picking through the ribs, my appetite suddenly stunted.

We finish off the boar—mostly Ram finishes it off— and find a shady spot to rest out of the sun. I'm not as tired as I have been the last few nights, partly because it's still the middle of the day and the sun is still up, and partly because I rested so well last night.

But mostly, I suppose, it's because my thoughts are still churning. I'm thinking about Ram and Ion, and how they're the same and yet different, and whether Eudora isn't maybe right after all, that dragons don't belong. And weirdest of all, I'm thinking about my children and whether having children at all wouldn't just saddle another generation with the same doubts and questions I currently can't answer.

Somewhere in there, I fall into a fitful sleep. At least, I think I'm sleeping. I'm reclining against a ledge of rock that props me up a bit like a beach lounge chair, so I can see straight ahead of me if I open my eyes.

The trouble is, I'm not sure if I dreamed I opened my eyes, or if I really did open them.

Ion is standing across from me, leaning against a tree, watching me.

And I get up and walk over toward him.

This has to be a dream, right? Because I know better than to do that in real life, never mind that I'm wearing swords at my hips and daggers on my thighs (I don't have the ones at my back, because that's not at all comfortable when you're trying to fall asleep leaning against a rock). But I have questions I want to ask him, and it's almost as though my subconscious dredged him up so I could quiz him.

Anyway, it's still daylight—broad, bright daylight. A butterfly flutters past me on the breeze, alighting on Ion's shoulder for a moment before fluttering on.

Ion speaks first. "You're too trusting, Ilsa."

My hands fly to the hilts of my swords.

"Not of me." Ion's smiling. Laughing at me? I'm not sure. "Of Ram."

"I'm too trusting of Ram? You're the one who tried to kill me."

"Correction: you tried to kill me. I was only trying to help you. I was *injured* trying to help you."

"Help me, how? By taking me to Eudora?"

"You don't have to go to her. It was merely a suggestion. You want free of who you are? She can help you, but only if you want her help."

I'm watching him closely, trying to decide. I don't trust Ion. He killed Azi.

"I'm sorry about your dog. If it's any consolation, I tried to move my sword out of her way, but she leapt too quickly."

"You were trying to hurt me. She did it to save me."

"I wouldn't ever hurt you, Ilsa. Don't you know that? You started it. You drew your knife on me."

My heart is thumping heavy in my chest. Ion is lying.

Surely he is lying. He has to be, because if he's not, then I owe him a big apology. I turn the conversation to the questions I want to ask. "Do you want me to be human, or a dragon?"

"I want you to be happy."

"As a human, or a dragon?"

"Whichever you want to be." He pulls away from the tree he's been leaning against, and takes a step closer to me. He's a sword's-length away now. "Unlike Ram, I don't have a preference. Or an agenda. I want you to choose for yourself."

My hands tense around my sword hilts. Ion hasn't come any closer, but his words stab me, cutting deep. "Ram doesn't—" I start to protest, but I choke on words that sound untrue.

"Ram wants you to be a dragon. He needs you to be a dragon. And why?"

"Why?"

"Has he told you why?"

"To protect my village?"

"Oh, Ilsa." Ion shakes his head, pitying me. "He hasn't told you?"

Has Ram been hiding something from me? I hate to think he would, but then again, he already has—he's hidden so many things, kept so many secrets. What's one more?

"What is it?" I ask, my voice no more than a whisper.

"You've been betrothed since birth to a dragon king."

"What?" I'm sure I heard him clearly, but his words can't be true. They can't.

"You're a female, Ilsa. That's all he wants you for."

"Who?"

"Your betrothed. Sorry, but I've never learned his

identity. Some old crusty dragon who dwells deep in the mountains. He's rich, though, if that's any comfort."

I shake my head. "No. That's—that's craziness. It's medieval." Even as I say the words, I recall what I read in the road atlas. In the remote parts of the mountains, the people live much as they did in medieval times. But still, it can't be right. "My father would have told me. Ram would have told me."

"Just like they told you who you really are?" Ion blows out a sardonic huff of air, along with a tiny puff of fire. A tendril of smoke rises from his mouth, its scent more burning incense than wood smoke. "It's true, Ilsa. I'm sorry, but it's true. Ask Ram."

I glance behind me. Ram is still sleeping several feet away. He looks exhausted.

"Later." Ion's words pull my attention back to him. He took another step closer to me while my back was turned. Now he reaches for my hand.

I start to move my hands out of his reach, but he catches them. Both of them. Holds my gaze with his eyes.

"You don't have to go through with what they have planned for you. I care about you, Ilsa. I know you don't trust me, but I *do* care about you, and I would take care of you."

My mouth drops open. I want to protest, but I don't know what to say.

Ion drops my right hand, raises his fingers toward my face, and ever-so-lightly caresses my cheek. "Beautiful Ilsa. Believe me—I will let you choose. I will let you be whoever you want to be."

"But, I don't know —"

"Take your time. Choose. I'll be following you, always nearby. If you need me, call my name, and I will come and help you."

I turn and look back at Ram. Which of these guys is telling the truth?

"Ask him." Ion has stepped close behind me while my back was turned, and now I can feel his words tickling my neck as he speaks. "Ask Ram what their plans were. They only want you for your eggs. They don't care about you. I care about you. I'll be waiting."

I turn around just as Ion has finished whispering the word *waiting*.

He's gone.

If he was ever there at all.

I peer into the woods, which are thin at this altitude among the mountains. Was he ever really here, or did I only dream that part?

A tendril of smoke floats past me, its incense scent familiar.

Maybe he was here. Maybe he's still nearby.

I slip back to my spot near the rock and settle back in to sleep. Or did I ever leave at all?

Chapter Seventeen

"Night has fallen, Ilsa. We should get going." Ram nudges my shoulder, waking me gently.

Sure, *now* I'm sleeping hard, a deep dreamless sleep that weighs heavily upon me as I try to shove it away and rise past it.

"Want a bite to eat before we get going?" He holds out a roasted bird of some sort. Pheasant, maybe? It's hard to tell once it's roasted.

I sit up straighter, take the bird, chew a few bites, and swallow. "Ram?"

"Yes?"

"Can I choose who I am? Can I choose to be human?"

"If you never change into a dragon, then yes, I suppose you'd be human by default." He tears meat with his teeth, thoughtfully chewing. "But your DNA would still be the same, you know. You'd still be part dragon, even if it was latent dragon."

"What about my children? Would they be dragons?"

"Depends on their father, I suppose. If you married a man—a man who was only a man—your kids would be something in-between. I've never known anyone who was half dragon, but I've heard of them. Legend says Alexander the Great's father was a dragon."

"Really? But didn't you say he was one of the conquerors who targeted dragons?"

"Maybe he was trying to prove himself to his father." Ram suggests.

But I've already thought of another possibility. "Maybe he wanted to destroy the part of himself he didn't like, and conquering dragons was the only way he knew how to do it."

Ram frowns. "That might explain Eudora's genocidal fixation."

Though I can tell Ram is against the idea, still, I can't shake it. I don't want to be a dragon. That's not the same as wanting to kill all the other dragons. It's my identity, my choice. "What if I choose that? To stay only human, always. To live like a human?"

Ram sighs. "It's going to take longer to get you home."

"What if I don't want to go home?"

Ram breathes out heavily. I can't see his face in the twilight, so for a moment, I think maybe he's upset. But he rises as far as his knees, and kind of scoot-walks the last few feet between us until he's at my side, close enough his shoulder touches mine. He sits a little sideways so he can see my face clearly, and his blue eyes glow softly in the darkness. "I thought you wanted nothing more in all the world than to go home?"

I look up at him and swallow a bite of pheasant. I don't know what to say.

"All summer you've been talking about going home. Wondering when your dad was going to come for you, asking where your home is. You just wanted to go home."

I'm watching him, trying to remember the long summer back in Prague. It feels like it was a world away, falling, as it did, on the other side of the great divide— my life before I knew I was a dragon, and my life after I knew.

But the words from my dream spin through my thoughts. Was Ion's visit real? Did his words mean anything, or did I dredge them up with my subconscious? I have to know if I'm ever going to decide who I can trust—Ram or Ion.

"What's waiting for me in Azerbaijan? Why is it so important for me to return? What if I never go back?" I watch his face carefully. I need to see if he shows the slightest sign of bluffing.

"Your father is there. You're the only family he has left."

"But my father visited me at Saint Evangeline's. Why can't I live somewhere else, anywhere else? My dad could visit me there. Why do I have to return to the village where I was raised?"

"I thought you wanted to go home."

I shrug, trying to act nonchalant, although my pulse is pounding so hard I can feel it in my neck, in a blood vessel above my eyeball, even. This is why I always lost at poker. I cannot bluff to save my life.

But for the sake of the truth, I have to keep going. "The way home is barred by yagi. I was just thinking, maybe it would be easier for all of us if I didn't try to get past them. If I just slipped off somewhere else for a while."

"You don't care about going home?"

"Is there any reason why I should?"

"Your family—"

"It's just my father, right? Or do I have other family I—" I was going to say something like *I don't know about* or *I need to know about*, but I can't do it. My voice chokes off, my throat too tense to form any more words.

Ram stares down at the last of the bird bones he's picked clean. Like me, he ate the smaller bones, crunching them down. Delicious. And a great source of calcium.

"I promised your father—" he begins slowly.

"Promised him what?"

"That I'd bring you home."

Right. Paid mercenary bodyguard, or something like that. I'd almost forgotten. I'd begun to think of him as a real friend. But a real friend would have told me the truth instead of waiting for me to hear it from Ion. Maybe Ion's my real friend. "What if you don't?"

Ram hangs his head. Something painful crosses his face. He isn't going to cry again, is he? It was okay that one time, because his dog died and anyway I was crying then, too, but I don't know if I can handle much more of the big guy crying.

I'm slightly worried. "What? Are you going to get in trouble if you don't bring me home? Or is there something more?"

"There's something more."

For a panicked instant, I don't think I can take it. I *don't* want to know. But I desperately *want* to know. I wish I knew already. I don't want to hear him say it. "What is it?"

"Your father doesn't want you to know. He wants it to be a surprise." Ram blows out a long breath, meets my eyes. His are glowing with something I don't recognize. It's not apology this time, at least. Hope, maybe? But that seems weird. He makes his confession without losing eye-contact. "You're betrothed to a dragon king."

Even though I saw this coming, or was forewarned in a dream, or maybe not a dream, or whatever, somehow hearing it from Ram on top of already hearing it and desperately wanting it to not be true, makes it a hundred thousand times worse. I leap to my feet and throw down what's left of my pheasant carcass. "The bloody hell I'm not!"

"Shh, Ilsa." Ram stands and tries to take my hand, but I'm more likely to pull my dagger on him than let him touch me right now.

"Crusty old cave-dwelling lizard king!"

"He's not that bad."

"Bloody, bloody hell." I glare at Ram as he tries to shush me. "Every girl dreams of being swept off her feet by a creepy lizard who's *not that bad!*" Yeah, that was sarcasm, in case you weren't sure.

But then it's Ram's turn to surprise me. He's laughing.

"What the bloody hell is so funny?" I know I've said some of those words already, but to be honest, I feel slightly better when I use them, so I keep using them.

"Nothing." He shakes his head. "Nothing is funny. It's all terrible, really."

"You've gone daft in the head," I accuse him.

"I have," Ram acknowledges freely. "I've been fearing all through this trip how you'd react when you found out, and now I've told you, and the pressure's off."

"But I bloody well the bloody hell am *not* going to marry anyone, especially not some ancient dragon geezer."

"Right." Ram sobers slightly. "Ilsa, do you really *not* want to go home?"

I make a face. "I don't know. I thought I wanted to go home when I was far away. But the closer I get, the more I learn that makes me want to run as fast as I can in the opposite direction." I'm not sure whether I should stay fighting mad with Ram, or if I should be glad that he actually told me the truth instead of dragging me off to the lizard king with no warning of the fate that awaited me. And maybe he would have if Ion hadn't tipped me off.

But he told me the truth. That part seems to stick out above the rest, especially given that it was my uber-secretive father who tried to hide the truth from me in the first place. Ram defied him by telling me. It's almost as though Ram's more on *my* side than my father's side. That's something.

Ram sighs. "Has nothing good come of this trip, then?"

I fling my arms wide, shrugging dramatically. "I found out my dad keeps secrets from me, but then, I already knew that. You? It's been a terrible trip for you. Your dog died, you've been attacked and pushed to exhaustion, and you're probably going to disappoint my father by not delivering his daughter."

"It hasn't been a terrible trip."

"Hasn't it? Your dog died."

"True. That was a blow. But don't blame yourself—she was very old. She went down the way she wanted, saving someone she loved. And I don't mind being attacked, or the exhaustion. Overall, I'd say it's been a great trip."

"You're being sarcastic," I accuse him, though I'm not sure. He sounds like he's being honest, even heartfelt.

"I've enjoyed myself immensely."

"You haven't."

"I have."

"What made the trip good?"

Ram grins. Remember, this is the guy who never grins, or only that one time when I got the hang of the butterfly maneuver to butcher the steaks and also, as it turns out, to decapitate the yagi. When Ram grins, it means something. I'm not sure what it means, but *something*, something big.

The moon is up, nearly a quarter full, so even though the sun has set, there is still light to see. And here in the mountains the air is crisp and clear. "You are bluffing, then," I conclude.

But he's still grinning almost like he can't help it, and he shakes his head.

I prod further. "There's been nothing good. It's all been bad to worse."

"All of it?" He asks, and now his smile is a knowing smile with a secret behind it, and he calls my bluff and I realize maybe there have been a few good things.

Like waking up on his shoulder this morning in the abandoned castle in the foothills. And the moment I realized he'd taught me the butterfly maneuver so I could decapitate yagi. And, all right, yes, holding tight to his back while he flew me through the starlit sky. That was magical.

But I don't dare tell him any of that, because it all had to do with *him*. I can't very well admit all the good parts were because of him—especially since I'm supposed to be mad at him for keeping secrets from me, and there's every possibility I might take up Ion's offer and run away from him yet.

"Ilsa? Anything good?"

"Maybe," I admit, quickly turning defensive, shining the spotlight back on him. "What was good about the trip for you?"

"Getting to know you better." He speaks the words clearly, his eyes on mine for only a fraction of the phrase, and then he ducks his head as though embarrassed and walks away.

I watch him kick off his shoes and peel off his shirt, getting ready to change into a dragon. Is it just me, or did he get suddenly shy?

Ram, shy? I guess I'd already figured out he doesn't like using words as much as he likes communicating with his face. But *shy*? He seems too invincible, with his massive muscled shoulders too wide to fit through doorways, and the rest of him, all strong and trim and so very fine looking in boxer shorts. He's a way better butcher than I am, and a way better dragon.

And his favorite part of the whole trip was getting to know me better? Getting to know me was enough to make up for losing Azi?

I review the trip in my mind. My favorite parts were all Ram. And maybe that's the thing that terrifies me the most about this dragon king plan. I like spending time with Ram. And I don't want to give that up.

I hoist my backpack onto my back and walk over near him. "Hey, Ram?"

"Yeah?"

"If we ever get to the village, am I going to still see you?"

Ram turns to face me and pulls his backpack on. He's looking at me, but his face is unreadable. "I come from another part of the mountains. My home is not far, less than half a day's journey by foot."

My mouth drops open and I'm about to protest that it's too far, and I don't want to be so far from him, but he raises his hand in that signal that says he has something to say. Rather than talk over him and risk that he might decide not to say these words at all, I remain silent.

Ram speaks. "When I spoke earlier, I was out of line.

Please forget I said that."

"Said what?" I'm nearly sure I know what he's referring to, but I want to be certain, and anyway, it seems weird that he would claim it was out of line for him to say he enjoyed getting to know me better. I mean, it's a nice, pleasant, un-offensive thing to say, right? Unless it hints at something deeper, which his embarrassment suggests it does.

Ram hangs his head, which is a tad ironic—I mean, this is the strong guy who can fly through the air with me on his back, can decapitate a dozen yagi in under a minute (not that I've actually timed him, but I bet he could), whose biceps are as big around as my thighs— and I don't have twiggy thighs. But he doesn't throw his weight around to get his way. And right now, he seems genuinely ashamed of stepping out of line.

"I said I enjoyed getting to know you. I should not have spoken so boldly."

"It's okay. I've enjoyed getting to know you, too." I expect my words to cheer him up, but he only looks more miserable. Why? Is the paid bodyguard not supposed to make friends with the princess? Is it dishonoring to the dragon king I'm betrothed to? Bloody dragon king.

"Let's get going. We should be able to fly as far as the Black Sea tonight."

I have a thousand things I want to say and ask, but Ram's right. We need to go.

"Can I try changing into a dragon again?"

"Do you *want* to be a dragon?" Ram asks the same old question I'm so sick of hearing.

But I've thought of something that might help. "Tell me how you felt the first time you changed into a dragon."

A wistful smile peeks out from behind his beard. "I was four."

"A little younger than I am," I note when he falls silent.

"I'd seen my parents as dragons before. They were strong, mighty, beautiful. I thought there was nothing better in all the world, no greater thing. I wanted so much to be like them, to be able to fly as they did. My father thought I was too young, but my mother said if he didn't teach me to change properly, I might do it myself some time and get into trouble, fly too high or get lost or something. So my father made me promise I would only change with him."

Ram shrugs. "I've told you the rest. He held my hands, pressed his forehead to mine."

As he speaks, Ram takes my hands, touches his forehead to mine, and I try to feel it—his excitement, the joy of a four-year-old who wants nothing more than to be like his parents.

We stand like that for how long, I don't know, when I open my eyes enough to peek. Ram's hands are still gripping mine. His arms are blue-tinged, his fingernails long like talons, tipped in royal blue.

And so are mine. My fingernails have grown long and sharp, and the flesh of my fingers is tipped in a violet hue of purple. I'm so surprised, I gasp aloud.

Chapter Eighteen

Ram opens his eyes.

My hands go back to normal, and so do his.

"I'm not a dud." I'm panting. Wow, that is exhausting—and I didn't really change, not much. "I was starting to change. I was doing it."

Ram's breathing heavily, too. He rubs his temples. "I was trying not to change without you. I've never transformed so slowly." He winces as though in pain.

"Are you okay?"

"Fine. I'm fine. Just a bit of headache. Did you want to try again?"

"Let me catch my breath." It's exhilarating, but also terrifying.

Maybe the terrifying part is why, when we try again, nothing much happens. Or maybe it's because of my exhaustion, which seems to have erased all the sleep I've gotten in the last two days, and the meals I've eaten, as well.

And I didn't even turn more than my fingertips. What would happen if I turned all the way? I can't imagine.

That doesn't help my fear.

So Ram changes, alone, and I climb onto his back and hold on tight, burying my face against his neck as he flies, my thoughts mournful as I wonder what lies on the other side of the Black Sea. But I don't have to worry about the eastern shore of the Black Sea until we get over the Carpathian Mountains to the western shore of the Black Sea.

Ion said he'd be waiting for me, that he'd help me if I need his help. And Ion was right about the secret Ram and my father were keeping from me—their plans to marry me to a dragon king. Vomit.

Too soon, we land, and I'm still undecided. The day is just beginning to dawn beyond the sea. Ram changes, exhausted, into human form, gasps something about going in search of food, and leaves me alone with my thoughts.

I'm not alone for long.

Ion peeks warily out from behind a rock formation. We're in a remote area, on cliffs that jut over the Black Sea. It might be picturesque, but it's also dangerous, with sharp rocks jutting up among the waves below.

I step toward him, hoping he can stay mostly hidden so Ram doesn't see him. "You were right about my betrothal," I confess in hushed tones.

"Sorry about that. For your sake, I wish it wasn't true. But at least now you know."

"Yes. At least I know." In some ways I'm glad I know, but I also suspect that was part of what held me back and kept me from changing to a dragon last night. I was so close.

"What are you going to do?"

"I don't know. I can't decide. I've only ever wanted to go home, but..." I chew my lower lip. I can't confess to Ion what I don't want to admit to myself—that I have feelings for Ram. I don't want to leave him behind. I feel safe with him, and understood, and even kind of happy. But if he's going to be half a day's journey away, and I'm going to be married off to some horrible lizard, what good will it do me to go home?

"It's not the same as going back to being a kid, is it?"

Ion gives me a look which I think is supposed to be sympathetic, but there's something disingenuous about it, almost as though he's trying not to gag on his own words.

"I didn't expect it to be." I shrug. "Look, Ram just went to find supper. He'll be back soon."

"We should hurry, then." Ion takes my hands.

I freeze. "Hurry?"

"And leave before he gets back."

"I never said I was leaving." I'm tempted to pull my hands away from Ion, but I don't want to start a fight with him. Not when I'm alone. He's bigger than I am, and a better fighter. But neither am I going anywhere with him, not against my will.

Ion hangs his head. It's similar to Ram's apologetic pose, but at the same time, I'm acutely aware Ion hasn't let go of my hands. He's not squeezing them, but his hold is tenacious, nonetheless. "They're going to marry you off."

"That's the plan, but—"

"We've got to leave before that happens. I can hide you where they'll never find you."

This thought is not comforting to me, but I don't say so out loud. I don't want him to think I want rid of him, because I know what happened the last time I tried to push him away. I've got to put him off, play for time. "Just wait, okay? We're going to stay here for now and rest. I'll talk to Ram. If I need your help, I'll find you. Okay?"

Ion looks like he's going to protest, to push his proposition further, but I hear Ram's voice as he returns from the hunt.

"I wasn't sure I'd find much, but I caught a brace of

ducks." Ram steps into the clearing holding headless waterfowl in both hands.

I glance back toward Ion, but he's gone.

"Are you all right?" Ram squints at me. "You look flushed."

"Fine. Tired. Need help with the ducks?" I've been glad to see Ram many times before, but never so palpably. Relief rushes to my head. Ram is back. Ion didn't carry me off. I'm okay.

For now.

"Peel 'em," he says, handing me a fistful of limp birds.

I set the pile on the grass and watch as Ram demonstrates the process — holding the loose skin around the neck, then pulling it back, down the body and over the feet.

"It's faster than plucking out the feathers," he explains.

I follow his example, finishing up the last of the birds as he begins gutting and then roasting the first. The roast duck smells great, but my stomach is still churning from my conversation with Ion.

Ram props a sturdy stick horizontally between two rocks. As he finishes cooking each bird, he ties their feet around the stick to keep them off the ground. In short order, he's flame-broiled eight ducks. "Eat."

I take a duck and pick at it. The meat is delicious, and I'm hungry, but my appetite is ruined by anxiety.

Ram finishes off his first duck before I've swallowed two bites.

"What?" Ram tips his face with concern.

The sun is up now and I can see his expression clearly. He looks tired, but also worried. About me? Most likely. Part of me says I should tell him about Ion's presence nearby, but another part of me thinks they'll only fight. Ram could get hurt. No, I took care of Ion for now. No need to start a fight.

And it's not like I'm short on worries to confess. "I don't want to marry the dragon king."

Ram had bit into another duck while I debated what to say. Now he chews and swallows. "Maybe you should wait until you've been introduced to him before you make that decision."

"Maybe I should have been introduced to him before anyone started making wedding plans."

"He's not an awful old lizard, or dinosaur, or whatever else you've called him. Don't vilify him until you've met him. Would your father set you up with someone awful?"

"My father sent me to live at Saint Evangeline's."

"Ouch." Ram stops gnawing on the duck and steps in front of me. He looks directly into my face. "Want me to tell you about him?"

"I don't know. Mostly I want him to not exist."

"Reserve judgment, if you can. He's a very nice king. His people are quite fond of him."

"Who's he king of?"

"A tribe of Azeris. In modern terms he would equate more with a regional governor, but his kingdom is what it has always traditionally been. He and your father would like to unite those kingdoms under one family."

"I thought you said dragons were fiercely territorial? They don't play well with others."

"Your father and your betrothed have decided to rise above all that for the sake of their people. They are neither ancient nor barbaric. But he is a valiant fighter, this groom of yours. Wise. Kind. He has a spectacular dragon-hoard of gold and jewels, including jewelry that would look very nice on you. He's a generous man who wants only to make you happy."

"And for me to bear his dragon babies."

"To my understanding, laying an egg is far less painful than giving birth." Ram shrugs. "Not that I've tried either. He's a fine man, Ilsa. I wouldn't deliver you to anyone less."

Those words are too much for me—the tenderness behind them, the affection even. I hand Ram the duck carcass I wasn't eating anyway, and step away from him.

I see a flicker of movement beyond the rocks.

Ion.

He's watching.

Waiting.

But Ram steps after me and places a hand on my shoulder. "Your father only wants you to be happy. He hoped you'd find the betrothal romantic. Arranged marriages are an old tradition."

"It's barbaric."

"According to that tradition, girls were given a choice."

"I haven't been given a choice."

"I'll give you a choice." Ram bends down so that he's looking me straight in the eye.

"What choice?" I can hardly get the words out. What choice is there, really? I'm supposed to bear dragon babies.

Ram makes a pained face and shakes his head. "Your father isn't going to like this," he whispers.

"What?"

"I don't want you to be unhappy. I can't stand the

thought—okay, okay." Ram seems to be making up his mind, convincing himself of something even as he speaks.

"I don't want you to get in trouble with my dad."

"I'd rather face your father's anger than know I had any part in making you miserable. Here it is, then. This is the best I can do. If you'll travel with me to your village, to your wedding—"

"Wait, *when* is the wedding?"

"The plan was to have the wedding as soon as you return to the village."

"But when do I meet my betrothed?"

"At the ceremony."

"What?" I take a step back, look about frantically, spot Ion among the bushes.

He looks ready to leap out to my rescue.

I wave him back in a moment while Ram has his eyes closed. Ram appears to be thinking, or trying to find words.

I know how much he doesn't like using words. He's so much better with swords.

"I will be there," Ram continues, meeting my eyes again.

"At the ceremony?"

"Near the front. Your father will escort you to your betrothed. If he does not meet your approval, if you sincerely feel you cannot marry him, come to me."

"Come to you?"

"I'll be there, close at hand. Take my hand and we'll go."

"Go?"

"Fly away together. Run away together."

"You'd run away with me?"

Ram looks at me with a look I can't describe, a look that's more than affection, more than desire. A look that says he'd face my father's wrath for me, fly away from home for me, that I'm all he's ever wanted, anyway.

I told you he was better with non-verbal communication.

I'm relieved, so relieved I can hardly stand up. And I'm happy. Crazy happy. Happier than I would have thought I could be, and I wrap my arms around him gleefully.

"Ilsa, no," Ram cautions me, taking a step back. His expression is this weird combination of fear and *guilt*? Can that be right?

It's only a quick glimpse. For one disoriented second I think he's still being prudent, keeping me at arms' length until he's delivered me properly to my betrothed, but then I see his hands fly over his shoulders to his swords, and this time he's shouting.

"Ilsa, no!"

I spin and reach for my sword just as the yagi fly at us in full force, their screaming wails reverberating palpably through the air. Ram's back presses to mine as we fly into action, fighting as though we were born to fight like this, back-to-back, as a team.

But even as the first yagi heads roll, Ion leaps toward me.

"Come!" he shouts, reaching for my hand.

"No! I'm not going with you!"

Doesn't he see? I don't need Ion or Eudora. Ram worked it out. We have a plan—an escape plan. Something better than an escape plan. Ram offered to run away with me. I don't care what the dragon king looks like. I'm going to run away with Ram and we're going to be blissfully happy. So there.

The wall of yagi parts as Ion approaches me. Ram is surrounded—fighting, fighting hard. But even as I try to keep my back close to his, the yagi slash at me with their talons and rapier horns. They're vastly creepier in daylight, if you can imagine it. Buggy eyes that stare, blank yet evil. Hands that are not so much hands as taloned insectoid claws. Spiny legs that look like they belong on beetles, not on men.

And worst of all, they're pulling me away from Ram.

"Ilsa, come to me." Ion reaches for me with one hand, almost like a gentleman offering to help a lady down from a pesky perch. It's as though he's offering to help me step unscathed through the yagi. But if he has the power to protect me from the yagi, why isn't he using it?

He's using the yagi to drive me to him, to drive me away from Ram.

"Stay away from her, Ion. She isn't yours."

"She isn't yours, either, Ram." Ion sneers.

"I'm not anybody's!" I shout over them, felling a couple more yagi, almost for effect, and kicking their headless bodies Ion's direction.

He dances over them with surprising grace and reaches for my hand.

"Stay away from her." Ram bars the way with his sword, still fighting yagi with the blade in his other hand.

But Ion has drawn his sword, as well, and blocks Ram's blade.

"Sorry, Ram." Ion laughs. "Ilsa and I made a deal."

"A deal?" Ram beheads a yagi and kicks it back into two others, toppling them like dominoes, though they stagger back to their feet again.

He glances at me, and blast it all, I look guilty. I know

I do. If it wasn't enough for me to feel the guilt burning on my face, I see clearly in Ram's expression as he recognizes it and realizes Ion's words were true.

No, no, no! He can't believe the worst of me. He can't.

"It wasn't a *deal*," I protest, slashing fiercely at the yagi, wishing they'd just back off already. But they're not going to back off until Ion tells them to, are they?

Bloody buggers.

"A *plan*, then." Ion sounds disgustingly casual and aloof. "Kind of like your plan, Ram. A plan to run away together. But we made our plan first." As he speaks, Ion slashes Ram's blade away (which he wouldn't have been able to do if the yagi hadn't been hounding Ram, but I've already figured out Ion doesn't fight fair).

In the same motion he swings the sword round at me, flicks my right-hand sword away (how does he do that? I hate that!), and grabs my arm, morphing into a dragon as he pulls away, toward the sky.

I am not going with him. I'm not! I slash at his arm with the blade in my left hand. He's growing so fast, I don't hit his body or even his arm so much as the forearm of his dragon arm, which is armored with scales not quite fully tough. If I'd struck a split-second later, when he was fully dragon, his armor would have repelled my blade. But since he's not quite fully changed yet, my sword pierces his nascent armor. Red blood wells through the cut.

His hold on me loosens and I pull my arm free, throwing myself back, away, far from him, stumbling over fallen yagi.

I scramble for a gap in the struggling mass, the only open air that's not solid rock or seething yagi.

"Ilsa!" Ram is surrounded by yagi, fighting his way

free, when I realize *why* there's an opening among the mercenaries.

I've leapt toward the cliff.

And now I'm falling, falling, with nothing to grab hold of and only sharp rocks among the waves below to break my fall.

Chapter Nineteen

The rocks are numerous and sharp, with not nearly enough space between them for me to land safely in the water anywhere, even if I could maneuver myself to land in such a gap, which I can't.

There isn't nearly time.

I'm falling far too quickly.

I can feel the sea spray on my face and arms when talons grasp me, pulling me out over the open water and then slowly up, fighting the still air with every beat of his wings.

For a moment I'm not sure who's got me—Ion or Ram—but then I hear a dragon scream and see Ion flying off the cliff after us.

And for all my relief at not crashing to my death, I realize we're doomed still. Ram was exhausted before he fought the yagi and changed again. Now he's trying to haul my sorry butt over the Black Sea, and Ion will be upon us in a moment. Ion will destroy him.

I can't let that happen.

But what can I do? If I could change into a dragon maybe I could be a help to Ram, for once, instead of being a burden. But I can only change into a dragon if I *want* to be one, and besides, Ram's already changed, so I can't change with him and I don't know how.

Something huge and tragic wells up inside me. I came so close to running away with Ram, to being with the man I love.

With the dragon I love.

The thought twists up from my heart to my head

even as I feel the heat of the flames Ion's shooting.

I love a dragon.

Because I love Ram.

And Ram is a dragon.

So then, I don't know, maybe it's because I'm jolly well certain if I don't do something immediately, Ion is going to kill Ram (they say necessity is the mother of invention), I try.

I mean, I try really, really hard.

Never mind that Ram isn't holding my hands to help me.

Never mind that I don't know what to do, or how to make the switch, and that it never worked before.

I am *not* going to let Ion kill Ram.

My fingers had at least changed that one time before, so I start from there, building on that feeling, visualizing the whole thing with a kind of desperate urgency that's stronger than just *wanting* to be a dragon. I *have to* be one.

Something weird happens, then. Ram was sagging in the air, beating his wings frantically trying to haul me over the sea, but then it's like I've broken free of his grasp, or outgrown him, or something.

And I open my eyes to see—I am a dragon.

A purple one.

Sweet.

I whip through the sky, swirling up over Ram, into Ion's face, intending to blast him with shooting fire.

And I scream at him instead.

Fire is apparently tricky.

But he looks seriously disoriented, so I take advantage of my position and claw at his face like I once saw a couple of bona fide princesses do to each other at Saint Evangeline's, when they got into a row over who's manicure was better.

That incident ended with both of them breaking nails.

This one results in me scratching some serious claw marks across the tender scales around Ion's face. Turns out my dragon nails are vastly more wicked than any princess manicure ever could be.

I feel a flicker of triumph before Ion recovers from his shock and shoots fire at me.

Blast it, that's hot. Remembering Ram's story about fireproof wings, I wrap mine around myself, which blocks the fire, but it turns out in this position I don't fly nearly so well.

Or, you know, at all.

I flap my wings again. Ion and Ram have sailed on ahead of me. Ion looks intent on attacking Ram, which worries me, because I know Ram was already zonked before he did several things which are sure to only tire him out further. So Ion could really hurt him this time.

Just like he really tried to hurt me.

I was foolish to listen to Ion as long as I did. I realize that now. In my defense, I didn't know who to trust, and everything was strange and new, and Ion was saying the things I most wanted to hear.

But now he's shooting fire at Ram, who's sagging in the air, knackered, too knackered to put up much of a fight.

I shoot toward them, flying as fast as I can. You might think I wouldn't know how to fly, having never done it, but it turns out the flying motion is the same thing as the butterfly stroke that slices steaks and beheads yagi.

Ram is bloody brilliant, and I love him.

The only difference between flying and beheading yagi (besides the obvious decapitation, of course) is that the move is done with my wings and not my arms. This is a tricky distinction, because dragons have both wings and arms. They share the same bone structure, the wings sprouting out of the scapula, while the arms stay where they always were (I figured this out while I was riding on Ram's back with lots of time to study his shoulders).

So to be honest, though I've got the flying maneuver down mostly, I'm not accustomed to having wings *and* arms, and I've never had the chance to practice using them independently, and now is not the time for that. All I care about is flying as fast as I can to catch up with Ion and Ram, and hopefully help Ram get away from Ion before Ram gets seriously hurt or killed.

Which means, as you may have guessed, that along with flapping my wings and flying through the air, I'm waving my arms a bit madly, because they move with my wings and I don't know how to do one without the other.

Fortunately there aren't many boats out on this corner of the Black Sea at this hour. I see one boat below, but I'm not paying it any attention. If the people on board have spotted us, they're probably wondering about the three dragons flying through the air overhead, and why the purple one is waving her arms frantically. Maybe they're even waving back.

But I don't have time to look.

I've almost caught up to Ram and Ion and now I've got to figure out what I'm going to do. I still have my swords strapped on (bloody brilliant of Ram to devise holsters that stay on when we change), but in order to get close enough to Ion to use them, I'd have to be within range of his shooting flames, his talons, and his swords.

Maybe I can shoot fire.

It can't be that tricky. Ram can do it in human form or dragon form. You'd think it would be a more introductory-level trick than changing shape, but no one's mentioned to me how it's done.

I come at them screaming. Technically I'm *trying* to shoot flames, but it's still not working. But the screams alone are pretty terrifying, coming, as they do, from the panicked part of my soul that's afraid Ram could die before I ever get to tell him how I feel about him.

Ion seems distinctly freaked out, maybe because he never really expected me to figure out how to turn into a dragon, or maybe because I'm so out of control furious that he's afraid I might actually hurt him even worse than I already have, which I am completely prepared to do.

And also maybe because he knows I've figured out he was lying to me, or at least feeding me whatever line he thought I wanted to hear, just so I'd go along with him—but now that I've seen through him there's no way I'll ever listen to him again.

So Ion kind of does this spin in the air, rolling around toward me instead of hounding Ram. And for lack of a better plan, I pull my swords from my hips and fly into him at full speed, screaming and flailing my arms (yes, I still haven't figured out how to keep my arms still while beating my wings) and generally trying to do as much damage as I possibly can so he'll leave Ram well enough alone.

For a few moments, it's bloody thrashing chaos. Ion claws at me with his talons, but I rip into him with mine, and I'm slashing like mad with both my swords, which mostly get deflected by the armor of his scales. Some parts of my body sting like maybe I'm getting hurt, but at this point I don't right well care. I've noticed he keeps trying to use the horns that grow out of the top of his head — we all seem to sprout these two horns when we change. They look extra sharp and it really hurt when one grazed me, so I try to avoid them.

Then Ion erupts with fire shooting from his mouth, and I shift to block the fire with one wing, while making sure to get between Ram and Ion again, because I don't want Ram getting hurt any more than he already has.

But Ion beats his wings and jets past me, shooting his fire past the shield of my wing, toward Ram, who whips around, snarling, rocketing upward with his wings curled inward, protecting himself even as he rises up into Ion's face, shooting fire back at him.

The flames meet in the air, so hot I can feel them billowing around me even as I wrap my wings around myself, spin, arch forward, and sail around in a wide circle, hoping to attack Ion while he's distracted with Ram.

I soar over his head and whip my tail down at him as I fly past.

The move sends him reeling, stunned, toward the sea.

Then I swoop around toward Ram, scared of what I might find. But as I approach him, he's still gliding, sagging a bit from exhaustion, but still aloft. The glow in his eyes says everything his words never could — that he's proud of me for figuring out how to be a dragon, and working with him to fight against Ion, and all that.

I give him a look back, one that I hope says I couldn't have done it without his help, and that I'd change into anything, if I could, for him.

Ram glances behind him, and I look, too, but Ion is gone.

Where did he go? Into the sea? Land is far, far behind

us (we were flying so fast, and it took me longer to catch up to them than it did to tell about it). Could he have gotten back to land so quickly? I don't know.

Before I can worry more about Ion's whereabouts, Ram droops in the sky until his toes graze the water, and now I'm more worried about what's going to happen to Ram than I am about what became of Ion. I don't know how Ram could possibly make it back to shore in any direction, never mind that the closest bank is the one behind us, a sharp cliff straight up with hordes of yagi at the top.

But Ram falls sideways, lowering himself into the sea on his back, his body sinking halfway in. He spreads his wings wide, floating there. Just floating. He looks up at me with a drowsy face that seems to question why I haven't done the same.

So I do.

It's a bit of a trick getting myself turned around backward, and then for some reason I'm crazy afraid the weight of my tail is going to drag me under, but once I tip my head back so my weight is supported by my wings, I realize they're kind of like a boat. A fire-proof, water-proof, flying shell of awesomeness.

Okay, so there are some brilliant bits to being a dragon.

Ram stretches out his dragon fingers toward mine, links our talons, and closes his eyes.

We float and sleep, holding hands so we won't become separated, which is important to me for even more reasons than usual now. The water is warm, bathwater warm, and the small waves lap gently, rippling beneath us. We're not quite weightless but nearly so.

I have no idea how long we've been floating, or

which side of the lake the sun is on, or where we are, or anything, but I get the sense the sun is more up than down when Ram squeezes my hand and I peek over at him.

He's holding up a fish.

Oh, yum.

We eat fish, lots and lots of raw fish as we pull them one by one from a school swarming beneath us, which I suspect may have been attracted to our glowing scales, not that it really matters why they're there. I'm just glad they are. I was insanely starving and the fish, in addition to being food, are also full of moisture, which is important because did you know the Black Sea is salty? I found that out when I got thirsty and tried to drink some.

But the moisture in the fish is enough to get us by, and I realize Ram has been slowly propelling us across the sea with wafting tail motions and toe flicks, or something, because we rest awhile longer, until darkness falls, and then he pulls my hand as he rises up out of the air.

In spite of mostly sleeping all day, I'm still tired. I'm completely unused to being in dragon form at all, let alone for so long, even if I was only eating and sleeping, my ponderous weight mostly supported by the saline sea.

It's not completely dark yet and I can see the shore ahead of us, twinkling with the lights of towns and cities, and judging from the fact that the sun is setting behind us, it must be the eastern shore.

I studied this section of Ion's road atlas. Georgia, Armenia, and Azerbaijan are squeezed between the Black Sea and the Caspian Sea, from west to east, in that order. So the shore I see is the country of Georgia, and we'll have to pass through, near, or over Armenia to get to Azerbaijan.

Home.

The place I've wanted to return to for so long.

I flap my wings just enough to catch the updraft of warm air as it rises from the surface of the sea into the cooling night sky. We glide lazily, neither of us bothering to flap our wings more than enough to keep us aloft and soaring east. The night is long and I may have dozed off several times during the trip, but Ram didn't let me wander or drift away, and soon the lights grow bigger, marking signs and streetlights and illumined windows.

I beat my wings a little harder. We're almost there.

But of course, the closer we get, the more I realize everything is inhabited here. There are cities stretching into cities. Town, villages, and resorts hug the coast. There's nowhere for a dragon to land.

Looming above the city lights I see the dark heads of the mountains—the Caucasus. Ram steers toward one of these dark shadows and I stick close to his side.

Cool air flows down from the mountains. It sweeps under our wings and we catch it, rising up, up, into the dense trees that cling to the outer fringes of the range.

Ram swoops around, low, hardly above the treetops. Then he finds a spot that meets with his approval and hovers there. He watches me carefully, like he's making sure I'm able to follow, and sinks between the trees.

I do the same, landing gracelessly, exhausted, as Ram turns into a man once again.

As I sink to my knees, ready to cry with exhaustion, I realize, too late, I have no idea how to turn back into a human.

I would cry if I had the strength. Instead I curl into

something like an exhausted semi-fetal position, and close my eyes and wish I knew how to be a person again, without this big heavy body that is seriously tough to haul around when it's not being supported by updrafts or all the water in the Black Sea.

Something soft touches my skin. I'm only vaguely aware of it, but it brushes my fingers so I pull it closer around me, then I realize what it is.

One of Ram's flannel shirts. His voice is gentle. "Exhale slowly, like you're deflating. Let all the dragoness out of your body along with the air. Breathe out until you can't breathe out anymore, and then squeeze and breathe out more."

I think he's trying to tell me how to become a human again, and I try. I really do. I breathe out all my air and keep exhaling, almost like a straining sob, like when you want to cry but your sorrow is too deep. I strain after that smaller form of myself until everything goes dark.

Chapter Twenty

The sun is up when I awaken. It feels early out, but it might only be cool and shady because we're in the mountains. Ram's roasted up a bunch of something delicious, and when he offers me some I take it and eat ravenously, still half asleep, realizing only once I've chewed it down to the bone that I'm still lying on my side, in the dirt, mostly naked except for Ram's big shirt draped across me like a blanket.

Also, I am human again.

It's a good thing Ram is big and therefore wears big shirts.

"I miss coffee."

"You'll be home tomorrow morning. You can have some then."

I didn't even realize I'd spoken out loud (I'm still partly asleep) until Ram answered me.

Now I'm aware of time again, and plans and things to do. "Do we need to leave soon?"

"No. Rest. We won't go anywhere until tonight. Then we'll fly home."

"What about Ion? And the yagi? They could catch up to us."

Ram shrugs. "I don't know what happened to Ion."

"I don't think we killed him."

"True, but he probably had to go off and bleed awhile, and gather his strength. Turning into a dragon is exhausting for him, too. Not just for us."

The thought is slightly reassuring, but at the same time, I hear a tone in Ram's brontide voice, an unfamiliar twinge of—could it be guilt? I remember the look he gave me in that fraction of a second before Ion and the yagi pounced on us yesterday. He looked almost guilty then, too. But why would he?

The act of talking and eating has worn me out, and I take Ram's advice and rest, but the question still bothers me, of why Ram looked guilty, and what he feels guilty about. If anything, I should be the one who feels guilty, because I let Ion into our camp and gave the yagi an opportunity to pounce. I almost got Ram killed.

I sleep on and off throughout the day, awakening now and then to the scent of roasted meat, eating only to sleep again, knowing I need my rest if I'm going to fly home tonight, because it wore me out so much the last time and I didn't even fly very far—just floated, mostly.

When I awaken to sunset I slip my arms through the sleeves of the big flannel shirt. Once I close the buttons down the front it's like I'm wearing a loose shirt dress. I have to roll the sleeves, but otherwise it's not a bad look, especially if I'm only going to change into a dragon again.

Once I'm decently covered, I stand up on my feet, which is a strange experience after being a sort-of four-legged winged creature for most of the day yesterday, and sleeping the day away. I feel a little wonky, like when I was a kid and I spent too long swinging on the swing in my backyard, like I'm no longer used to the solid earth, or it's not used to me.

I take a few steps closer to Ram and study his face. I'm finally rested enough to address the question that's been bugging me through my sleep.

"Hungry?" he asks me.

"I'm just trying to decide," I explain as I look into his

eyes, which have this sort of haunted look not so far back. At first it's almost like he doesn't want to make eye contact, but then finally he looks squarely back at me, and I'm sure of it.

Guilty.

Of what, though? It's troubling, because the last conversation we had before this look showed up, was when he offered that I could run away with him if I don't like my betrothed.

"What?" Ram asks.

Since I need to get to the bottom of this, and since I have a hunch what might be bothering him, I take a guess. "Do you feel guilty about offering to run away with me, because you'd be breaking your deal with my father?" I watch his face closely as I pose the question, but I see no confirmation. Maybe a little at first, but then it fades. Weird.

"I feel guilty," Ram confirms slowly, but then his voice breaks off and he shakes his head, sincere remorse saturating his expression. "I gave you an option...that's not really an option."

As I'm watching him, listening to him, dread and sorrow well up inside me. What's he saying? Is he saying we can't run away together after all? I *have* to marry the dragon king?

Ram pulls out a dagger. Its razor-sharp blade reflects the sun as he raises the edge toward his throat.

At first I'm just watching him, upset yet curious, not really sure what he's doing, but then he tips his head back and places the blade against the skin just below his beard.

"Ram, no! What are you doing?" I'm about to grab his arm and try to pull it away (not that I can reasonably expect to out-muscle him, but just because I have to do something) when dark hairs fall away.

There's no blood. I watch, transfixed, as he glides the edge of the dagger up his neck and over his chin.

Long black beard hair drops in thick clumps. His skin underneath is brown like mine, but not quite as brown as the skin on his arms and the parts of his face exposed to the sun.

It takes a little while for him to get his beard all shaved off. I watch him, particularly nervous when he shears the hair from his upper lip. As he works, his face is revealed to me one swath at a time. I've been curious, ever since he was a talking beard with goggles, to see what his face looks like exposed, without the beard.

Part of me kind of figured maybe he was ugly. Like he wore the beard to cover his face. Maybe he was scarred or had a scrawny chicken-neck he didn't want people to see.

None of those guesses are correct.

Ram is gorgeous. Think of the most handsome man you've ever seen, and double it. No, triple it. All I can think is, maybe that's why he wore the beard — so he wouldn't have women falling at his feet all the time, or modeling agencies trying to sign him.

But he still looks like Ram.

And he still looks guilty.

I remember, then, what he'd said just before he took out the dagger — that the option he gave me wasn't really an option.

As soon as he's finished shaving and puts his dagger back away in its sheath, he explains, "I didn't expect you to be so happy when I told you we could run away together. I just wanted you to feel like you had an option.

I didn't think you'd actually take it."

I want to demand he clarify. I want to scream. But my throat feels tight and I figure no amount of screaming or demanding will hasten his explanation.

Ram continues, "When you looked so happy, I realized what I'd done wasn't fair. It hadn't occurred to me that you'd actually want *me*, when you could have a king. And then Ion showed up, twisting words and saying the two of you had made plans—"

"Those were Ion's plans, Ram. I never agreed to them."

"I believe you. Ion does that with words sometimes— makes the honest, ugly and the truth, untrue. He can be deceptive. I've always resented that about him. But at the same time, I realized—that's exactly what I'd done, in giving you an option, in saying you could choose between me and the dragon king."

Ram hangs his head, almost shamefully.

My heart is bludgeoning my insides with its painful pounding. What is Ram trying to say? I'd hung my only hope of happiness on his offer to free me from the marriage agreement I never agreed to. He *can't* un-offer it.

But it sounds like that's precisely what he's doing.

"Ilsa, I'm sorry. My words have deceived you. And I apologize in advance, because I'm going to break the promise I made to your father. I told him I'd keep this truth a secret above all else, but I see now, secrets are a close cousin to lies, and I won't have either come between you and me."

Ram takes my hands and looks at me earnestly. "The truth is, you can't choose between me and the dragon king. I am the dragon king."

For a minute or two, I just stare at him. Partly because, did I mention he's stunning? I'm still getting used to this. I might have to get used to it for a while.

And partly because I'm digesting what he's said. There's a distinct disconnect between his tone of apology and my sense of excitement, so I'm trying to rectify those two. "So, you're apologizing because you've misrepresented yourself?"

"Yes." He looks at me warily, with maybe a twinge of hope behind his blue eyes.

"But the truth is, I'm engaged to marry *you*?"

"Yes." The twinge of hope grows.

"So, how do you feel about that?" I'm still trying to get to the root of his apologetic tone. So far I've only found good news.

Something wistful crosses his face, almost like a happy memory has just gone dancing through his thoughts, and I can see it if I look deep enough in his eyes.

"I want to marry you," he acknowledges. "I'm just not sure how you feel, marrying a crusty cave-dwelling dragon-lizard."

For a second I don't know what to say. Those were my words, weren't they? Pretty much spot on. "*You*," I start, gesturing broadly with one arm and drinking in the sight of him, "I want to marry."

That wistful happy look grows.

I continue, "But, I mean, you're the dragon king, valiant fighter, treasure trove hoarder, and all that. Surely you have females lining up — "

"None of my exact species."

His words are a reminder of why we're marrying. There's just me for him. It's me or nothing. Which makes me feel slightly sad on his behalf. He has to marry me, the least of all the princesses at Saint Evangeline's. "Are you disappointed?"

"Why would I be?" Now he looks sincerely confused.

"You thought you were getting a dragon princess, but it's just me."

The confusion is replaced by something like offense, like somebody's insulted his favorite cut of beef. "*Just* you?"

"I'm not very princess-like." I hasten to explain. "And I'm not much of a dragon, either. I wave my arms when I fly. And I can't breathe fire." I could elaborate about my defects, about my weird-colored eyes, and my solid build which always made the scale-reading school nurse shake her head in dismay, and the fact that Ram is so much better than I am at so many things, but he's shaking his head emphatically and holding my hands.

"I didn't want you to be like those fragile princesses in the brochure about Saint Evangeline's. And you fly amazingly well for your first time out—you flew across the whole Black Sea on your first try."

"I floated most of the way. That's rather cheating, I suppose."

He ignores my correction. "You're more than I dared to dream of, Ilsa. How many princesses would butcher in a refrigerator for twelve hours a day, all summer long? I love the way you *try*, even when you can't see how something's going to work. And how you fight for the things you believe in, like your right to go home. And the way you eat a steak." Ram gets this sort of hungry look on his face. "I love the way you look when you eat a steak."

"I love eating steak."

"I love that you love it." Ram looks like he might say more, but I've heard enough. I'm ready to go.

Now.

"Right." I can't quite smile or jump up and down gleefully on account of that disconnect, and also because I did that yesterday when he offered that I could run away with him, and then Ion jumped out and tried to kill Ram and kidnap me, so I'm keeping my reaction subdued this time, and also I'm still maybe a tiny twinge in denial. "We need to get going."

"Where?"

"To the village. To the wedding!"

A whisper of relief crosses his hairless face, and it occurs to me that, for a guy who always talked with his face and not his words, suddenly his expressive vocabulary has expanded far beyond what it was before. I can see his lips now.

And they're crazy hot.

I feel this overwhelming sense of urgency, not just because I want to marry Ram and I want him to be the dragon king, but because I feel a horrible sense that this is not going to work out.

Maybe it's because every time I've gotten my hopes up—that my dad would take me home, that Ram and Ion would drive me home—everything I've hoped for has been jerked out from under my feet and I've fallen and gotten bruised and had to claw my way back up, with literal claws, even.

Call me jaded or just realistic, all I know is, this is why Ion has been hounding me—because he doesn't want me to marry Ram. And Eudora doesn't want me to marry Ram. And now that I'm close, *this close* to happiness, so close I can see its face and it's a hot face because it's Ram's face without the beard…I know, I just know, they're never going to let it happen.

Ion and Eudora are going to stop this. They'd kill us before they'd let us have dragon babies together.

So all I can think is that we have to hurry, fly faster, get there before them, marry before they can stop us.

Even though all my instincts and everything I've learned tells me they will stop at nothing to prevent this marriage from taking place.

Ram must sense it, too, because he's not protesting. He stripped down to his boxers already and he's securing his backpack and his swords.

I've got my swords on at my hips and my daggers on my thighs, but I'm not sure about putting on my backpack and swords over my flannel shirt dress. "Your shirt is probably going to get shredded when I change."

"It's okay. I have other shirts." Ram's words are matter of fact, but the tone under his words and everything in his face says it doesn't matter if we shred a thousand shirts, we need to get going.

This does not reassure me.

"Something else I thought of when I saw you fighting Ion." Ram talks quickly, squeezing in the information before verbal discussion is no longer possible. "Dragons are armored, you know—our scales are essentially impenetrable, except for the softer scales on our undersides—belly, underarms, inner thighs. It's nearly as tough, but it can be pierced by dragon horn."

"Dragon horn?" I repeat.

"The horns on the tops of our heads—they're the toughest weapon I know of, sharpest, too. The only thing that can pierce dragon armor."

"That's why you flew under Ion and gored his belly

with your horns."

"Precisely. Our horns, talons and tail spikes are the few effective weapons that *really* hurt another dragon. It's tough to kill a dragon that way, though. Even the horns are too short to reach the heart. Ready?" Ram asks, and takes my hands.

"Ready." In spite of my fear, I'm more than ready. I'm eager, not just to get on with our journey and get to our wedding, but to be a dragon again, because to be honest, it was pretty fantastic. Exhausting, heavy even, and terrifying, but also amazing in ways I can't describe. Because I could fly. And float like a boat. And, theoretically at least, breathe fire.

"How do you breathe fire?" I ask, now that I'm thinking of it, because if my hunch is correct I may need to use that skill before long.

"It's a lot like singing."

"Like *singing*?" I'm surprised by Ram's answer, not only because I wasn't expecting him to say that, but also because I've never heard him sing, nor can I imagine him doing so.

But sure enough, with a bit of a sideways smile that says he's happy to teach me, and maybe even glad I asked, he explains, "It's like when you sing a high note. You've got to raise the soft palate at the roof of your mouth. Do you know how to do that?"

"Yes." Back at Saint Evangeline's we were required to sing in the choir for at least one semester. The director was adamant about teaching us good technique and all the physiology behind it.

"Like so," Ram opens his mouth, and then belts out a falsetto *aaaah* that's actually pretty impressive.

"Aaaaah!" I echo him, in the same key and

everything.

"Precisely. Just do that when you're a dragon, and you'll breathe fire."

"But you can breathe fire as a human, too."

"True, but that takes a bit more practice." He winks at me, turns his head to the side so he's not aiming his mouth my direction, and then, making the same face he just made to sing falsetto, he breathes out a billow of orange-tipped flame. Then he closes his mouth and turns back to me. "We should get going."

"Thanks for taking the time to show me."

"I'm glad to. It's a skill you might need." An undercurrent of danger runs through his words, and he glances at me, a quick check to see if I heard that note and if I'm worried.

Of course I did, and I am. I raise an eyebrow just a twitch.

Ram closes his eyes, dips his head slightly to apologize for frightening me, and then admits, "I believe there is still danger ahead of us. Also, you should know, in case things happen which I fear may happen, your father is a scarlet-orange dragon. Eudora is yellow, a sickly yellow tinged with green."

He has that look on his face again, the one I saw in my hallway the night Azi first started growling, the one that says this strong, nearly-invincible man, is worried.

Maybe even scared.

Chapter Twenty-One

Changing is not so difficult this time, though it's still a monumental effort and I'm not sure I could have pulled it off at all if Ram hadn't been holding my hands, pressing his forehead against mine. And then we fly through the night over the mountains. Ram sets a gentle, gliding pace, so that we reach my village just as the pre-dawn light is beginning to color the eastern horizon.

We land in the King's Tower, which I remember from my childhood, a tall, medieval stone tower with high parapets surrounding the flat top, shielding the deck above from the sight of anyone below. I always just figured the name was an ancient one, not a clue to my father's true identity. I haven't seen the tower in over a decade, but it hasn't changed, and I instantly recall memories I hadn't thought about in years.

My father used to come down from the tower after trips, whenever he'd been away. He'd enter the city through the door in the base of the tower, dressed in a long, flowing robe.

As a child, I'd assumed that was normal, because that's the way he'd always done it. But now I understand how unique and significant his entrance was.

Ram changes first. He's still in his boxer shorts, and he explains the procedure to me, pointing. "There are doors — men's, women's." He gestures to each in turn, on opposite sides of the round tower. "You'll find a robe in there. Put it on, go down the stairs. I'll meet you at the bottom."

I nod my purple dragon head and Ram ducks away

through the door. I'm alone. It's not a comforting feeling. I want so very much to be human again, and get through the tower and be reunited with Ram, but I don't know how to change.

Yet, even as I want it, and think to myself how very much I want it, and deflate my breath like he taught me, I see that my arms are brown again instead of purple, my fingernails rounded instead of sharp claws. I duck inside the door, slip into a robe, and hurry down the stairs as though someone might be just behind me, chasing me.

Ram is waiting for me in the large room at the bottom. "Ready?" He takes my hand.

I slip my hand into his and nod, exhausted and ready for a nap or a meal, preferably both. He's acting as though stepping through the door is a big deal, and I suppose in some symbolic way, it is—my return to the town of my birth, to the people I was born to protect.

But it's not yet morning, not really, and I expect we'll slip into town quietly, without anyone noticing.

In that, I was wrong.

Ram opens the door and we're greeted by a loud cheer, which startles me out of my drowsiness and makes me think somebody should have told the villagers to keep it down, or they're going to alert the yagi to our arrival.

But then, if Ram is right and Eudora has spies among us, I suppose it doesn't matter if we're quiet or loud. She'll know soon enough either way.

Villagers have lined up all down the central street that runs through town, just as they used to flock to the roadside to welcome my father. Back then, I never minded the crowd because I was always so excited to see my father. Now it's a tad disorienting, especially considering the sun's only just coming up, so it's not fully light out, and I'm zonked from being a dragon.

Thankfully, Ram has firm hold of my hand and guides me down the road. We're both in flowing robes like my father used to wear—Ram's a giant cloak-like garment that wraps all the way around him with an extra draping fold that covers his shoulders, a rich navy blue jacquard that's vibrant and regal.

I had grabbed the first thing my hand touched that felt right, which turned out to be a teal and white paisley print with highlights of magenta, but it's at least a sturdy cotton fabric instead of some of the flimsy chiffon things my fingers rejected at first brush. It fits like a wrap-dress, with a tie belt at the waist to secure it closed and adjust the size, and it makes me feel slightly feminine for the first time since I started being a butcher.

People are waving and cheering and even throwing down leaves and flower petals, like a ticker-tape parade, but more organic. Ram waves back, looking every bit like a real king should, kind of reminiscent of the way my dad waved to his people when he entered the village.

So I wave, too, even though I don't recognize anyone.

I mean, I don't recognize *anyone*. The buildings are the same, the tower was the same. I know we've got the right place, but was I really gone that long? Ten years?

We've walked about a block and I'm starting to get worried again, that maybe I was gone too long, and home was just a dream, and it will never be the same, when I spot the first familiar face I've seen.

And it's not even human. I mean, it's sort of pseudo-human. It's a doll, the embroidered cloth doll face like my friend Arika and I used to play with. This one is being held by a tiny girl who looks barely old enough to stand on her own, maybe two years old at most. And the crowd's kind of pressing close to us anyway, so I step toward the little girl as we move forward.

When I reach her, I crouch down and look at the doll.

The girl looks at me with round eyes. She doesn't seem afraid of me, but she's watching me carefully. I smile. "When I was a girl, I used to play with a doll like this. But I don't remember her name."

"Tulip."

"Tulip. That's right!" I stand, coming eye-to-eye with the little girl's mother, who's also holding two babies — twins. But that's far from my biggest surprise.

"Arika?"

My friend smiles, and I recognize her, in spite of the ten years that have passed between us.

"Welcome home, Ilsa." When she speaks, her English strong but accented, I remember in a rush things I hadn't thought about in years. Like the fact that I grew up speaking Azeri until I was eight years old, which is why I remembered that *yagi* means *enemy*, even if I've forgotten most of my native tongue. I also recall that Arika and I learned English together, taking lessons from a tutor who came to my house. The reason Arika learned the language was so I'd have a friend to practice speaking with, besides my father, who spoke English well.

On some level, my father must have always known he was going to send me away to Saint Evangeline's. That's why I had to learn English.

But all those realizations come in an instant. I smile at Arika in wonderment, taking in the changes. She's taller and more mature now, of course, but she also has children. Three of them! Granted, I seem to recall she was a bit older than I was, maybe even a year or two, but that would only make her nineteen or twenty at most.

And she has three children.

Ram squeezes my hand and we keep moving. I wave back at Arika and smile, and she and her daughter wave happily back, but inside me, my exhausted mind has kicked back on, mulling thoughts I hadn't thought to think.

Arika has three kids. Granted, twins are not a common thing, but still, that could be me in another couple of years. Will be me, if the dragon-babies plan comes true.

I glance back, over my shoulder.

Arika looks happy. Her children look happy.

I pass the rest of the walk in a daze. This is craziness, you know, the plan for me to marry and have children. I'm eighteen years old. I don't care if dragons are nearly extinct, and if they need me, and if it's perfectly normal, even expected, to marry young in my native village, where life continues more like it did a thousand years ago than today.

We reach the stoop of the house where I grew up, a pale yellow stucco house that's taller than most of the others in town, with blooming plants cascading from the second floor balcony, their vines encircling carved stone columns, filling the air with fragrant scents.

My father is watching from the top step, but comes down to greet me, scooping me into his arms. "You were supposed to wait for me to come get you! What happened?" He sounds pleased to see me, but concerned, just the same.

"Ion brought a message that it was time to leave. He said you'd sent him."

"I did not. I would not." My father straightens

suddenly and looks at Ram solemnly. "Ion is no longer welcome here." He shakes his head and turns to me. "Events of late have made it impossible for me to leave."

I glance around at the village, which seems so peaceful, full of flowers and villagers scurrying back to their work.

My father clears his throat and leans close to Ram, speaking in a hushed voice. "Eudora is a crafty one. We've rooted out three of her spies in the past two months. I wouldn't be surprised if there were more. She knows Ilsa is coming of age, and she's frantic to stop our plans from progressing. Speaking of, what does Ilsa know of what's to come?"

I turn back from looking at the village, and watch my father and Ram carefully. I know Ram can communicate perfectly well without words, especially now that his face is uncovered, and I wouldn't be surprised if my father shares his talent.

Ram lifts both eyebrows in a gesture like surrender, and my father looks surprised, then glances at me.

Just as I suspected, they're talking without words. In spite of my exhaustion, I'm alert, watching them carefully, unconvinced they've shared all their secrets with me.

"How much does she know?" Father whispers. Perhaps he suspects I can read their faces as well as they can read each other. In the case of Ram, I very nearly can.

"Of the wedding? Everything."

"And of Eudora's plans?"

"She knows as much as I know—that Eudora intends to prevent our union. She's bent on eliminating dragons from the earth—judging from the number of yagi we've slain on our way home, she's quite determined."

"Hmm." Father's lips twitch as he listens to Ram's report. I realize now, looking at him, that he doesn't look any older than the last time I saw him or the last time I was in the village, or ever. And yet, according to Ram's claim, my father is more than 200 years old. I can almost see it in his eyes, which are a startling bright scarlet-orange.

"How much trouble did the yagi give you?" Father asks.

"We managed," Ram says simply.

"The yagi weren't as bad as Ion," I offer. "He kept trying to drag me off."

Father nods sharply. "That's it. That's her plan. The yagi were just a distraction. Not that they aren't dangerous, of course. But they were mostly there to keep you busy so Ion could deliver Ilsa to Eudora."

His explanation fits with what my instinct told me all along. "Why is Eudora so determined to get her hands on me?"

Ram and my father exchange worried looks.

"What's the latest word?" Ram asks in hushed tones.

"My spies say it's ready. She hasn't been able to test it, of course. That's why she'll stop at nothing to capture a test subject."

"Me?" I guess in a whisper. Maybe I'm picking up on their non-verbal cues, or maybe it's just because of my limited knowledge of Eudora, but I suspect that whatever it is Eudora wants to test, it's probably related to her experiments that ultimately killed my mother.

Whether it's the thought of that, or simply the fact that I've been walking and standing for far too long in spite of my utter exhaustion, I slump against Ram unsteadily.

He props me up, half hugging me, half carrying me as he climbs the steps and guides me through the front door. We sit, exhausted, on a sofa, and I lean against Ram while Father runs to the kitchen, returning with coffee and the promise of meat.

I clasp the warm cup with both hands, letting the heat seep through my fingers as I sip.

"We should get you to bed," Ram suggests. "You need to sleep."

I shake my head. "The wedding—"

"Won't be until this evening at the earliest." Father finishes my sentence. "Until then, rest is the best thing for you."

"I'll rest after I've eaten. Until then, tell me what Eudora's up to. Please. I'm tired of secrets."

Something passes between Ram and Father. I'm too drowsy to catch it all—most of my attention is focused on raising my coffee cup to my lips without spilling any. But I think Ram communicated, in that effective wordless way of his, that my father *does* need to tell me everything.

I'm grateful he's finally on my side on that issue.

Father clears his throat. "It's a serum. For decades Eudora's been working on a serum to change dragons into humans. She thought she had it figured out nineteen years ago when she sent word throughout the dragon world that she could transform anyone from dragon to human."

"Wait—the dragon world, what is that?"

"Dragons and their supporters," Father explains. "Everyone in my kingdom and Ram's kingdom is part of the dragon world, even though only the three of us are dragons. The dragon community has traditionally been connected through messengers who travel from one village or island to the next, sharing news. It's not known how many actual dragons there are left, because most of them live in hiding, their true identity kept secret for their safety. Your mother was one of those. Those closest to her were aware of what she truly was, but she didn't let on to outsiders."

"So, a messenger brought word to my mother that Eudora could transform dragons into humans, and…she went?"

Pain crosses Father's face. "This is the cost, you know, of living in hiding, keeping the secret of who we really are. She felt so…alone. Her parents were long gone, killed in the battles against dragons centuries before. She had her kingdom, yes, and they loved her, but she had no hope for the future, no children, no reason to keep going. She believed—strange as it may sound—that dragons no longer have a place in this world. That we should have all died off long ago, buried with our legends and heroes of old. That she'd been passed over. And this was her chance to rectify that."

I could tell him that I don't think it sounds strange, not strange at all, but I don't want to interrupt his story.

"So, she went to Eudora, to her fortress deep in the wilderness of Siberia. But even before Eudora attempted to use the serum on her, Eudora shared with your mother her ideas and philosophies, about destroying all dragons, about ridding the kingdoms of the dragon world of their protectors. Your mother began to doubt whether she'd made the right choice. In fact, she started to think perhaps we dragons ought to try harder to work together—that we've feared one another far too long, but should instead band together, united by our common dragoness.

"But when she told Eudora she'd changed her mind, Eudora flew into a rage. They fought—your mother fought to escape, but she was alone and Eudora had all her yagi to help her. Eudora chained her in her dungeon. She would have used her serum on her, but your mother stayed in dragon form, and she couldn't inject it, not past her scales. It wasn't for lack of trying, though.

"Fortunately, I'd been keeping a close eye on Eudora ever since her announcement. I feared what she might do, and rightly so. When I learned what was happening, I traveled there personally to help your mother escape.

"She was in very rough shape—her wings torn, her body bruised. Eudora had been merciless. We managed to escape, but your mother was not strong enough to travel far. I kept your mother safe for as long as I could. We fell in love. She laid your egg. You were her every hope, her every dream for the future. She made me promise that I'd keep you safe—that even if she had to die—" Pain cuts off Father's words. He takes a shaky breath and concludes, "You'd be safe. She'd live on through you and your children."

Chapter Twenty-Two

I'm dumbfounded by Father's story. Not that there are too many surprises — Ram effectively told me the gist of it. But hearing it from my father, who lived it and loved her, something settles in the pit of my stomach — the determination to see her dreams fulfilled, to carry on her legacy, and all that.

Father brings in meat and we eat while he finishes his explanation. "Eudora still wants to use the serum. She still wants to defeat the last of the dragons, to purge the earth of us."

"That's why Ion was trying to capture me, instead of just killing me?"

"Precisely."

"Why didn't Ion insert the serum into me? He's had plenty of opportunities."

Ram clears his throat. "Eggs?"

Father looks thoughtful. "Faye told me everything she could recall about Eudora's plans, about her philosophies. Eudora claimed she wanted to destroy all dragons, but she also tried very hard to convert Faye. It was almost as though she wanted a follower, more than she wanted to destroy her."

"And look at Ion," I point out between bites of meat. "She could try out her serum on him, if she really wanted to, but she hasn't."

"She always said the best weapon against a dragon is another dragon," Ram reminds us.

"You know that old saying, 'if you can't beat them, join them?' One of the girls at Saint Evangeline's used to turn that around. She'd say, 'if they won't join you, beat them.' Think maybe that's Eudora's philosophy, too? She wants us to be on her side, but failing that, she wants us dead?"

Father raises both eyebrows. "I think you've got it. But what's her plan?"

"And how do we stop her?" Ram adds.

I don't have an answer for that, and I've finished my meat. Ram helps me to my childhood bedroom—which, I realize now, is in the center of the house, not only the most secure location in the house, but arguably the most secure in the whole town. Father took seriously his promise to my mother, to keep me safe, didn't he?

I barely make it to the bed before I fall into an exhausted sleep.

*

I awaken to wedding preparations in progress. Whatever Eudora's up to, no one seems willing to let her potential plans get in the way of my future happiness, or my matrimony. I bathe and wash my hair properly for the first time in a week, and step into the gold and white lace gown that appeared in my room while I slept.

The face in the mirror is me but not me. I look older, or bonier, or something. Not skinny. Just more mature. My cheeks less round, more womanly. If that's a thing. And most notably, my eyes have turned a jewel-toned amethyst color that fits me better than the ruddy brown before.

Mahira, a woman who helped take care of me when I was young, who was elderly then and who has visibly aged since I've been gone, arrives to braid my hair, weaving ribbons and jewels into the plaits. And then Father appears. He looks distinguished in a traditional embroidered suit.

"Is it time?" I ask.

"Not yet. I only came to see you because I couldn't wait. I've missed you." He gives me a hug. "They're still setting up chairs in the village square. Ram's tribe has been invited, and they're trying to squeeze everyone in. It's a very large crowd."

"Any sign of Eudora?"

I expect Father to pat my hand and assure me that all will be fine, but instead he looks concerned. "Some villagers traveling from Ram's tribe have reported seeing yagi in the mountains. No one has been attacked or hurt, that we know of, but it would seem she's on the move."

"What are we going to do?" I smooth down my dress, which is lovely, but I feel so exposed without my swords. "I need a weapon. Should I wear my daggers under my dress?"

Father might have laughed off the suggestion, but he doesn't. "Good idea. The ceremonial swords will be on the table with the rest of the symbolic weapons, in front of the wedding bower. Ram will be wearing his swords. If it's any help, I think Eudora would rather capture you than kill you. I don't know if she'll try to use the serum on you, except as a last resort."

"You mentioned she couldn't use it on mother when she was a dragon, because of her scales?"

"Yes. She used a needle-syringe. It won't penetrate our scales. We're armored, except for our eyes and inside our mouths. Keep your mouth shut and your eyes guarded, and you'll be fine."

"What about the villagers? Is it wise to let the crowd gather when there could be danger?"

"Our villagers are all drilled in evacuation plans.

There are many exits to the caves accessible from the village square. We're passing this information along to our guests. But I don't think we need to worry about the people, except to get them out of the way of flames and swords and yagi. Eudora has never shown any inclination to hurt people. It's only the dragons she's concerned with."

Father meets my eyes solemnly. For not the first time since I've been back, I notice his are a bright scarlet-orange, vividly jewel-toned, which is not how I remember them. "Your eyes used to be a reddish-brown," I murmur, not intending to change the subject or even speak out loud.

"I covered them up with contacts when you were little—anything to keep us hidden. But there's no point covering them now. You know where I am. So does Eudora. I don't know where we're going to hide you if she arrives while you're still here."

"What? Still here? Where am I going?"

"Back with Ram to his side of the mountain. It's only a short flight from here, but he's got a more secure fortress. I tried to hide in plain sight, you know, nothing too fortified—I didn't want to attract suspicion. He took a slightly different approach. If Eudora knows you're around, you'll be safer there than here. But where to hide you if she shows up before then, I don't know. I'd send you into the caves with the others, but what if she follows you?"

"I won't endanger the people."

"There's the tower, I suppose," Father continues thoughtfully.

"Why should I hide?"

"To keep you safe."

"Why can't I fight her?"

"No, no—"

"I've fought Ion and the yagi. I can defend myself."

"Ilsa, please. Be sensible. You are the last hope of the dragon world. We can't endanger you in any way." He knits his face into an expression of resolve. "The tower, then. It's the only secure place where you can be sure you won't endanger innocent civilians. If Eudora attacks before you and Ram leave town, flee to the tower. Promise me?"

What is it with my dad and promises? I am not a coward who turns my back and runs. But he doesn't know me, or doesn't know the eighteen-year-old me. Only the eight-year-old me. I haven't had a chance to show him I can defend myself.

And now is not the time. So I nod, the same nod I've seen Ion and Ram use, the deferential, almost-a-bow nod. "I may have to defend myself on the way to the tower," I warn him.

"Yes, of course." He's smiling now. He wants me to be safe, and I've agreed to his plan, and now he's happy. We step through the house toward the front windows, and he looks outside to see how the wedding preparations are coming along.

I look, too, but my thoughts are not on the hundreds, even thousands of chairs being set in rows in the square. I am thinking of how I might defend myself from Eudora without breaking my promise to my father.

It's a tricky question to answer, because I don't just want to chase her away. If I'm going to be laying eggs or bearing dragon babies, or whatever, I don't want to have to worry about her swooping in now and then to try to kill them or carry them off. I don't want to live in fear anymore, or fight this battle any longer than I have to.

The simple solution would be to kill her. Isn't that how enemies have defeated one another for long centuries? And she's the one who thinks all dragons should die, so it would be a fitting end, never mind that dragons are all but immortal.

But it sticks in my throat that if I kill her, I'll only be proving she was right — that dragons are killers. That we don't know compassion or mercy. That we don't belong in this modern world, but are relics of a brutal past.

You know I almost sided with her when I first found out about dragons. I feared I was a monster, and I didn't want to be a monster. I still don't want to be a monster, or a killer. I didn't want to be a dragon, either, until I realized I'm in love with a dragon.

So I'm torn. I want to get rid of Eudora so she won't be a threat to me or my family or my people any longer. But I also don't want to kill her, because on some level that would make me no better than she is. I want to be a dragon of love, not a dragon of death.

But I don't know how to do that.

*

"Ready?" Father holds out his hand to me.

I'm not. I'm not ready at all. I still haven't figured out how to defeat Eudora without becoming a killer like she is. I'm not even sure if I'm ready to marry Ram. Come to think of it, we haven't even kissed yet, or anything, which is a grave oversight on my part and probably only due to our having been dragons, or scarfing down meat, or half-dead asleep for most of the time since I realized I love him.

Although in retrospect, if I'd thought of it, I could have tried kissing him while I was eating, or something.

That might have been right fine.

And I'm not sure I'm ready to bear dragon babies, even if egg-laying isn't as bad as giving birth. Arika, my friend from childhood, has three kids. She can handle it. She was always better with Tulip than I was. I'm not ready for this.

But I place my hand on Father's elbow, anyway, and give him a smile that's totally bluffing because nine-tenths of me is terrified and about to run away. And my father places his other hand over mine and smiles at me like he's proud of me, although honestly, what have I done today besides my hair? And technically I didn't even do that, Mahira did.

Still, when I think of Ram and the fact that we'll shortly be married, and then I can make up for not having kissed him yet, I'm ready. More than ready.

So between the parts of me that want to run away and the parts that want to sprint down the aisle between the chairs in the village square, I manage to walk at a reasonable, solemn pace. Ram is standing at the front, under the wedding bower, near the table with the symbols of our union, including a sword, a bow and arrows, and a round shield.

He's watching me walk toward him, and his eyes, which usually sparkle like jewels, are lit up with eagerness. For all his skills communicating without words, right now he's sending me a message, as clear as if he was shouting from the rooftops. That he loves me. Me, just me, Ilsa. The butcher. The dragon. I don't have to hide who I am or pretend to be something I'm not.

Father and I reach Ram, who's standing in front of the table of symbols, below the wedding bower, which is covered with fragrant flowers of all colors, but mostly purple with highlights of blue, and just a few twinkles of orange and yellow for contrast. Father places my hand in Ram's hand, and he gives my fingers a gentle, reassuring squeeze.

We state words that bind us together, vows that bind us together, and sign the paper on the table in the midst of the symbols, the one that confirms we are husband and wife. For that moment, I'm happy, so crazy happy I could burst, and the whole world seems to fade away, and the huge crowd of people seems to fall into sacred silence, like they're holding their breaths, and I remember the thing we haven't done yet, the thing I've been waiting for, which will surely happen any moment.

I look at Ram eagerly, ready to kiss him for the very first time.

Then the screams erupt, and I turn to see that everyone is pouring out the sides of the aisles, evacuating quickly, even as the yagi overpower their screams with their inhuman wailing. The yagi leap from the surrounding rooftops, and two fire-breathing dragons swoop down from overhead.

"To the tower!" Father leans close as though he's afraid Eudora and Ion will hear from the sky. He clamps a hand on Ram's shoulder. "Take her!" Father shouts to Ram even as he transforms into a scarlet-orange dragon and bounds into the air.

The yagi rush toward us, toppling the bower.

Ram pulls out the swords on his back and swings his blades at the head of the swarm. There's no way we're going to get to the tower, or even out of the square, without killing some yagi first.

I've got my daggers under my dress, but those are for close-range fighting, and I don't want to have to get that close to the yagi and their spearing antennae. Weapons are spread out on the table like a feast of defenses, and I throw a bow and quiver of arrows over my shoulder. I haven't shot a bow since archery season ended last spring, but they're light and who knows what I'll need before I reach the tower.

There's only one sword, but it's a big one, and I grab it with my left hand, glancing up to see my father fighting Eudora in the air, while Ion dives toward us, breathing out fire.

I grab the shield and hold it over me to block the flames. As Ion swoops past and the fragrant flowers melt and burn from the heat of his flames, I shout to Ram, "He's going to burn down the village if we don't stop him!"

"I'll fight him!" Ram shouts back. "Get to safety!" He beheads two more yagi before leaping into the air, morphing into a dragon as he soars through the sky after Ion.

Ram did a good job of clearing out many of the yagi on this end of the square, and the people evacuated quickly. I run back down the aisle, toward the main street Ram and I just walked up that morning, when we were greeted by townspeople tossing flower petals.

I'm almost to the street when I hear a tiny scream, and I turn to see a little girl peeking out from under one of the many chairs that crowd the square.

She can't be more than two years old, if that. Though her dress is fancier than the one she wore this morning, I recognize her, just as I recognize the doll she's carrying.

Tulip.

Chapter Twenty-Three

The yagi have seen the toddler, too.

While technically I don't think yagi are supposed to bother humans, these particular yagi don't look like they're familiar with that rule, and no way am I taking any chances. I leap at them, bounding over chairs and performing a one-armed butterfly maneuver while I bar their way to the little girl with my shield. It takes me a little longer than usual to decapitate them all with just one hand.

"Jala!" Anika screams, running back into the square. I can only assume she evacuated with her babies, thinking her daughter was at her heels, only to realize once she got to safety that Jala wasn't with her at all.

"Mommy!"

Two more yagi are drawn to their cries. Jala looks at her mother with longing, but appears to be rooted in place — probably by the paralyzing screams of the yagi.

I'm moving swiftly, ignoring their screams, propelled by my own momentum.

I pick up Jala with my arm that's holding the shield (no, this is not a graceful move, and she's probably going to slip out of my grasp if I have to go very far, but I don't have much choice at this point) and I decapitate the two approaching yagi as I deliver the child to her mother.

"Thank you, Ilsa!" Anika cries as she embraces her child.

"Hurry! Get her to safety," I tell her, aware the paralyzing wails of the yagi might lock her in place if she stays still too long. Anika runs with her daughter while I decapitate another yagi and look up to see how Ram and my father are faring in the sky.

The village is not on fire, at least.

That's the good news.

Ram and my dad are trying to push back the dragons, but Ion and Eudora seem determined to fight their way past them.

Mindful of my promise to my father, I run down the street toward the tower. Along the way, yagi come at me from all directions, darting around buildings, leaping off rooftops, doing their best to slow me down and bar my way. It's exhausting, fighting them, but at the same time, I keep thinking of what my father said, that they're more a distraction than a worthy foe, in spite of their screams and venom and claws and horns. Granted, if I lower my guard at the wrong moment, they could very well fell me, but I can't help thinking they're not the real enemy.

There's something more going on, isn't there?

I check the sky again, but this time I can only see my father and Ion. Where's Ram? Where's Eudora? Somewhere out of sight, beyond the trees or the mountains?

Hopefully Ram has chased her far away, or better yet wounded her so gravely she'll never return.

I decapitate two more yagi, and as they fall, I can see the tower only a few dozen yards ahead. I charge toward the wooden door. If I can just reach it, and duck behind it—

A woman runs around a building, headed toward me. She's not screaming. She doesn't even look Azeri. Her hair is long and blonde, with maybe a tiny tinge of green, the same color as her eyes.

I'm about to run past her on my way to the tower

when she calls out to me.

"Ilsa! I've been looking for you. I want to help you!"

For one confused millisecond I think maybe she knows of a hiding place or something, but before that thought even fully forms, I realize she's holding a gun—a weird-looking gun with a big glass tube-looking thing on it.

She's coming closer to me, still talking. "I can help you. You don't really want to be a dragon, do you? Dragons don't belong in this world. You can be so much more."

She's talking in that uber-soothing tone like Ion used the other night. There may have been a time when I would have stopped to listen to her, but that time has passed.

I ignore her and make a run for the tower door, glancing back to see her hold up the gun and take aim at me. I block the shot with the shield as I reach the tower, haul open the door, and duck inside, slamming the drop bar behind the iron catch plate just as the woman on the other side throws herself against it.

It's Eudora, isn't it? Of course it is. There's a small glass window near the top of the door, and I can see her yellow-green eyes, a jewel tone somewhere between citrine and peridot, which I only know about because some of the girls at school were seriously into gemstones.

Also, her eyes look angry.

But even as I realize that, I look down at the round shield in my hand, which is made of wood covered in leather or something like it, and I see there's a syringe sticking out of the shield.

So that's what she shot at me. It's the serum—the serum to make me only human, and not a dragon anymore.

Suddenly I'm terrified and look myself over to make sure she didn't fire another one and hit me anywhere. But I don't see anything or feel anything, and it occurs to me that dart-guns are probably single-load, not a revolving multi-bullet-chamber like a regular gun.

I look back at the syringe in my shield. It didn't inject the serum, probably because the wood is hard, too hard for the serum to go anywhere, unlike porous flesh.

Outside the door, Eudora has changed into a dragon and is blasting fire at the door, which is made of thick, heavy beams. It will take a while for them to burn through, but they *will* burn. And given the heat of dragon fire, it might not take as long as I'd like.

I look at the syringe and then at the dragon outside as she takes a step back and gathers her breath for another blast.

She can't shoot me with a dart gun when she's a dragon, I don't think. Dragon fingers are too big to pull triggers.

I'm worried about Ram and my father and the rest of the village. I need to get out there and help them. If I wait around inside the tower, pretty soon Eudora's going to burn the door down, or she'll figure out she can reach me via the top, or something.

I need to act *now*. The syringe is sticking out of my shield, looking far more innocent than I know it to really be.

An idea, probably not a good idea, but the only thing I have, forms in my mind, and I tug a ribbon from my hair.

I pull a sturdy arrow from the quiver on my back (fortunately they're not just for show, but real arrows capable of shooting straight) and then I set the shield flat on the floor with the syringe sticking up, and I position the arrow next to it, wrapping the ribbon tight around the two, weaving them securely together.

The syringe is going to mess up the arrow's flight-path, of course it is, but I've dealt with something similar with our flaming arrow exhibition shoots at the Highland Games. I've even shot flaming arrows into moving targets, which was probably good practice, because I doubt Eudora's going to stand still.

I'll only have one shot. And I'll have to take it quickly. I'd aim for one of her eyes, but she could too easily blink and block it. Even if I make the hit, she could pull the syringe out or even claw out her own eye before the serum soaks in if she realizes her choice is to go through life minus an eye or only human.

That leaves her mouth, which will need to be open, wide open, enough for the needle to make it past her fangs. I'll have to make the shot as she's breathing fire, preferably when she's just opened her mouth so the blast hasn't grown to full strength yet, or it could incinerate the syringe and the arrow both, and then I'll have to come up with a new plan.

Once the syringe is tied tight to the arrow, I pull them both out together, taking care not to touch anything near the tip of the needle because no way do I want any of that stuff getting on me. My people and my future family need me to be a dragon.

But they also need me to get rid of Eudora.

She's between fire blasts now. I raise the drop bar, peek out the door, and see her gathering herself to spray another billow of flames.

I get the bow ready, the arrow nock fitted to the

string, the syringe on the outside. I test its weight with my fingers and estimate how much it will weigh the arrow down on the short flight path to Eudora's mouth.

Eudora's eyes light up like she's about to blow.

It's now or never.

I open the door partway and, using the door as a shield, duck past it just enough to get the shot off. Eudora opens her mouth and I take aim, watching the fire gather deep in her throat even as I let the arrow fly.

Then I duck back behind the door, slam the drop bar down behind the catch plate, and peek up through the glass.

The sickly yellow dragon is staggering back, her eyes round and rolled back in her head. She's pawing at her mouth, her throat, and I catch a glimpse of fletching sticking out of her mouth as her body seems to shrink away, receding.

I'd love to stick around for the show, to see how well my plan worked, but even if I did everything right and she shrinks back to human, she'll still be after me. And she'll have fingers that can pull a trigger then.

For that reason, I don't feel it's safe to dart outside and attempt to run past her.

I race up the stairs to the top of the tower, peeling off my wedding gown because it's really too nice to let it get torn to shreds as I morph into a dragon. I toss it aside on the stairs as I climb, and focus on turning into a dragon, which I'm still not very good at.

But I really, really want to be a dragon right now. I *need* to be a dragon. Ram and my father and my people need me.

I burst through the door at the top of the tower and unfurl my purple wings. Dropping the weapons where I can fetch them if I need them later, I leap between the parapets and take to the air.

Below me, Eudora is shrieking and spitting blood, but she's not a dragon anymore.

She may never be a dragon again.

I fly back toward the town square, scanning the horizon. Where's Ram? My dad? Ion? They're stonking big and bright in dragon form, so they shouldn't be too difficult to spot.

I see smoke rising up from a building near the square. Since the village is built on hard mountain rock where it's difficult to lay underground pipe, a lot of buildings have their own water towers on their roofs. I fly over to one of these, lift it carefully from its perch, and dump the contents on the flames.

Then I return the vessel because, let's face it, at this point I'm just flying in circles looking for Ram or my dad or any other fires that need to be put out.

The village is eerily silent, and I'm starting to wonder if maybe I should check the caves or something. I'm starting to worry, too. Remember how, when Ram first told me he was the dragon king, and I was engaged to marry him, and happiness was possible and all that, how I suddenly felt certain it couldn't work out, that something would go wrong and all my hopes would be jerked out from under my feet like always?

Yeah. I can't help thinking this is it, then. The happiness-jerking moment I've feared all along. Then I hear a cry and see Ion flying back toward the village from the other side of the mountain. He's surely seen me but he doesn't make any move to attack me.

Maybe he's looking for Eudora, but that's the least of my worries right now. Because beyond the craggy cliffs that jut up around our village, from the other side of the mountain, the direction Ion is flying from, smoke is rising.

Where are my father and Ram? Are they over there? Are they hurt?

Panicked, I fly toward the smoke. The mountains are little more than sheer jutting rock thick with treetops in between. I can't see anything but rock and trees, rock and trees, and then—village.

The rooftops are similar to those in my hometown, but this place is more fortress-like, with stone walls surrounding the village itself and many of the larger dwellings. There's a series of concentric circles fanning out from the mountain, and tucked in the most secure point, carved in parts from the mountain itself, is a fortress. A castle.

And smoke.

I fly closer and I can see orange and yellow flame, and then my father's orange dragon back bent over something sapphire blue lying in the courtyard. Father has a big white sheet of fabric something, and he's tugging it over the dragon, almost like the way they cover corpses in movies to signal they're dead.

I don't want it to be Ram. I really, really don't want it to be Ram, because it's not moving, and there's a dark red pool growing around it, more blood than we spilled in a day at the butcher shop. And it's all coming from the dragon.

It's Ram's blood.

Chapter Twenty-Four

I fly like a streak and land in the courtyard, running as I land until I'm next to Ram. My father gives me a haunted look, drops the sheet, and flies off.

I want to shout at him not to worry about Ion, but what do I know? Maybe he should worry. I grab the sheet and lift it up, realizing a number of things all at once. One, I've turned back into a person. Two, Ram is still breathing, though they're shallow breaths. And three, my father was apparently trying to use the sheet to bind the wound, or something, because now that I'm close I can see it's twisted around Ram's arm and chest. Dark red blood is soaking through it.

"Ram! Can you turn into a human? Maybe I could put a tourniquet on you if you were human." But even as I make the suggestion, I wonder if it's true. Can you put a tourniquet on a person's chest? What would that stop the blood flow to, anyway — their head or their body? Neither of those are probably a good idea.

I'm no nurse. I'm a butcher, which is quite near the exact opposite of nurse. But it also means I'm not usually squeamish around blood, except for when it's the blood of the man I love, and it's spilling from his body.

I have to stop the blood flow. Father's improvised bandage job doesn't look like it's doing the trick anyway, and tons of extra sheet are just hanging off doing nothing, so I take one of the daggers from my thighs and use it to slice a bunch of the sheet free, and slice a long strip like a bandage. Then I wrap the rest of the sliced-off sheet around my chest like a bath towel, partly to keep it off the bloody cobblestones of the courtyard, and partly because, other than my daggers and the torn remnant of the slip I was wearing under my wedding dress, I'm naked.

Okay, now for the scary part. I gingerly lift up the wad of blood-soaked sheet that my dad had stuffed over the injury, and inspect the wound underneath. There's a ton of blood, but I don't see any particular major vessels that need to be sewn back together.

While I'm inspecting it, a shadow falls over the courtyard, and I look up to see Ion flying past with Eudora in human form on his back. She looks rather pale and limp, but she seems to be holding on of her own volition, so I don't think I hurt her that bad.

My dad's flying after them, blowing fire their way, not so much like he's trying to engage them in a fight, but more like he's trying to tell them to go away and not come back.

I see all this in a glance and then return my attention to Ram's injuries. I'm not sure if I should attempt to sew the gash shut, but I don't have anything to sew with, and right now I just want to put enough pressure on the injury to stem the bleeding. I press the bloodied sheet back over the injury and then bind it in place with the long strip of cloth, wrapping it around and around as tightly as I can, and when it's all wrapped up, tucking the end underneath the previous layers.

While I'm busy with that, Father flies out with a water tower and dumps it on the part of the fortress where the smoke was rising. Steam billows up, but he seems to have taken care of the smoke. He lands beside me and transforms into a human, with some scarlet-orange pleated shorts on that I can only figure he had made for the express purpose of leaving him less than naked when he transformed back from being a dragon.

"How's he bearing up?" Father asks, his face pale with concern.

"I don't know. I tried to bind his wound, but it should really be sewn shut, I suppose. What happened?"

"Ion gored him with his horns. There's not much in the world that can pierce a dragon's armor. For that reason, you won't be able to stitch his wound until he's human—although I agree, stitches would help."

I nod. Ram had explained to me that our softer underbellies are strong enough to resist most weapons, but I hadn't thought about them being needle-proof, as well. Too strong to allow for healing stitches, but not strong enough to resist our own horns. We're our own greatest enemies. And Eudora knew it.

"Ram?" I step around near his head and place my hand on his dragon forehead. "Can you change into a human? I think it might help."

But Ram doesn't respond, doesn't open his eyes or give us any indication he's still with us at all.

Father puts his hand on my shoulder. "I'll fetch a healer to come have a look at him. If you can get him to change, they'll have a much better chance of helping him. It will take some of his strength to change, but once he's changed, his body won't have to work so hard to support him. He'll be able to pour his energy into getting better." With that, my dad turns back into a dragon and flies away, leaving me alone with the dragon version of the man I was so close to marrying.

This feeling is too similar to what I felt digging Azi's grave. Hopelessness, helplessness, a loss so big it smothers me. I can hardly breathe.

"Ram?" I'm not sure if he can hear me — probably not, but I have to talk anyway. There are so many things I haven't had a chance to say, and might never get a chance to say, if I don't say them now. Ram has always been the strong one, the invincible talking beard who knew all the secrets but wouldn't tell me, who was in charge while I sometimes followed along, but mostly opposed him.

But now I'm in charge and he's the weak one. If Ram had been mortally wounded a week ago and I'd had to do something to try to save him, I don't know what I would have done. Freaked out and called the Jitrnickas? I would have been absolutely undone, because Ram was the one link I had that connected me to my father, my homeland, and everything I am.

As a dragon, Ram's head is big — bigger than a horse's head, as big as my torso. His chin is resting on the cold cobblestones in a sticky pool of his own blood, but his forehead is quite a bit higher than that just because of his sheer size. And I sort of kneel in front of his face and hold on to the sides of his horns (which are smooth and rounded and not dangerous — it's only the pointy tips of the horns that are sharp) and I press my small forehead against his big blue scaly one, and I explain things to him as fast as I can sort them out.

"You need to become a human now, Ram. You really do, because if you don't, the healer won't be able to sew your wound up, and you'll probably bleed to death. And I don't want you to bleed to death."

By this point I'm totally sobbing because guess what? Today was supposed to be my homecoming and my wedding day, the happiest day of my life. And even if I wasn't one hundred percent sure and for certain I was completely ready to get married and start making dragon babies, I also know I didn't want the day to end like this.

So my tears are running down my face and splashing onto his face, and I just keep going, reduced to a sobbing mess while my dad tries to find a healer, which could take a while I suppose since the whole village was hiding in the caves, and the healer might even be busy healing other people. But I try not to think about that as I sort through the big soggy mess of my emotional state.

"I don't want you to bleed to death because I love you. That's different than needing you. A week ago and all summer before that, I needed you. You were my ticket home. You were the door and the key to my homeland, and going home was the one thing I thought I wanted more than anything."

About that point I stop talking, because making words takes a lot of effort and I'm pouring most of my strength straight through my forehead into Ram, as though I can make him turn into a human the same way he tried to get me to turn into a dragon.

And besides that, I realize Ram was never into verbal communication anyway. So I just mull my thoughts and sob my big fat tears onto his face, and realize how far I've come.

I found out I'm Azeri, but that doesn't make me who I am. It's part of me, and nice to know, but it didn't change much, not really.

I found out I'm a princess, too, which is something I might have almost wanted to be, way back when I first started school, until I got to know some of the princesses and found out their title didn't make them any better than anyone else. In fact, sometimes they acted like it gave them an excuse to be selfish and mean and petty. I intend to be the best princess I can be, but it doesn't make me who I am.

In fact, this whole trip has been a lot like butchering a carcass, except I'm the carcass. Things I thought were important to me got cut away. Like I thought my home was important, or my ethnicity, or whatever, but being here hasn't made me whole. And I thought maybe there was something between me and Ion there for a bit, but he was only ever trying to use me.

And Azi. Or Ozzie, however you want to spell her name. She was important to me. So important. She was comfort and understanding. She kept me from being alone. And she saved my life.

And she got peeled away, the shank from the brisket, the arm roast from the chuck, and everything got whittled away. Everything I cared about or thought I was.

And now Ram is getting cut away, too. I realize it with a horrible sense of loss, along with the bittersweet knowledge born of all the other losses I've been through.

I know I can survive.

If Ram dies, I'll be okay, just like I kept going after I lost Azi, and all those other things that cut away my image of who I was and replaced it with something unfamiliar.

In the end, at my heart, I know who I am.

I'm Ilsa.

I'm a dragon.

I'm a butcher.

I'm the protector of my people, just like the wedding symbols said. I'm the keeper of the fire. I don't *need* Ram to make me who I am or take me home, any more than I need my home to tell me who I am.

And so I tell him that, through choking sobs. "Hey, Ram? It's okay if you're tired and you have to go now. I want you to know you've been a gift to me and I treasure everything you are and all you've taught me.

"But you know what else? Even if I don't need you, even if I can still live without you, I *want* you to stay and be my husband. I want you to live because that would make me happy. And I think I could make you happy. We could share our happiness together and be the keepers of the fire and the protectors of our people.

"And Ram? If you want to make dragon babies, you're going to need to turn human first, at least for a little while."

So then my sobs turn into this tear-soaked blubbering, with warm memories, gratitude, and loving feelings bubbling up inside me, choking their way past the sadness and getting caught in a bittersweet tangle of uncertainty, desperate hope, and premature grief.

Even that's not nearly as picturesque as it sounds because, as you probably know if you've ever cried your heart out for a long time, pretty soon all those tears start to flow down through your nose like a flushing toilet, swilling out all the snot and boogers and slimy nose gunk, which just sort of runs on down your face with the tears.

And in my case, runs down Ram's face, too.

But as you might guess from the way Ram eats and belches and goes around splattered with blood all the time, he doesn't seem to mind the slimy nose gunk.

In fact, I almost think he likes it, because it's right about then that he turns into a human again, just in time for the healer to show up, riding to the rescue on my dad's back along with a couple of assistants and their doctor's bags and all that. And they try to shoo me away.

I don't want to go, but before I can protest, Father analyzes my slimy nose gunk and tears that are still globbed and dripping from Ram's face. "Oh, good — you cried on him."

"That's good?"

"Some say the tears of a dragon can grant wishes, even make miracles happen. Others say that's just a myth." He winks at me and leads me away so the healer can get to work.

I don't think I can watch Ram suffer for a second longer, and I have blubbered out every tear in my head, so I let my dad give me a tour of the fortress. (That may seem cold and unfeeling of me, but I'm emotionally spent, a shell of my usual self, plus I'm pretty tired from being a dragon and fighting and all that. I just have to get away and breathe.)

It's a wicked-cool fortress, with thick stone and tapestries and a state of the art kitchen with butcher's-block countertops, and as Father explains, it's all mine — mine and Ram's, anyway, if he survives. The fire damaged a section of roof, but my dad seems confident we can fix it.

When we get back outside again the sun is setting, casting that sort of golden glow across everything and making Ram look not so deathly pale, and the healer gives her prognosis.

"If he can make it through the night, he should live. He wouldn't wake up for us, but if he does, try to get him to drink water and eat something. That would be the best thing for him."

They've got him all hooked up to an IV, which looks pretty high tech here in the mountain fortress, and they transferred him off the cold cobblestones onto a stretcher. Between the five of us (four holding each corner handle and one bringing the IV bag hoisted high on a stand), we manage to lift him gently off the ground and carry him inside, to a bedroom that's bigger than my whole flat back in Prague, with lofted ceilings so high a person could easily change into a dragon without having to worry about having enough headroom or getting tangled in the chandelier. All the doorways are extra huge, too.

We settle Ram's stretcher onto the middle of the bed, and he doesn't twitch or even breathe very deeply.

So then while the healer and her assistants go back out onto the balcony to pack up their things, my dad gives me a hug and tells me everything is going to be okay, one way or another, which is not the most reassuring speech I've ever heard, but its more than my dad usually says.

Then he adds, "I'm sure the two of you want to be alone, and I need to get back to the village and make sure everyone is okay."

I nod dumbly. Normally, yes, I'd love to be alone with my husband on our wedding night, but considering he's unconscious, being alone together seems overrated. Still, I can't argue with the fact that my dad needs to look after his people. And I'll be okay.

It's Ram I'm worried about.

Father heads for the door in a hurry, then spins around and snaps his fingers. "I almost forgot. Ram said something about your wedding gift. It's in the bathroom. You might want to take care of it." He points to a door and then, while I'm looking at the door wondering what kind of wedding gift goes in the bathroom, my dad scurries away, calling out something over his shoulder about coming back in the morning to check on us.

And then we're alone.

I look at Ram. He's still awfully pale, but he's breathing, and his bandages haven't bled through. That's something, at least.

Since there's not much I can do for him, I head over to the bathroom door and open it cautiously.

The bathroom is massive, all marble and travertine, the middle of the room dominated by a huge soaking tub that would probably fit a dragon or two, and a chandelier that looks almost like a waterfall. For a moment, all I can think is that Ram gave up this place for his flat in Prague, which I never went into but judging from the outside wasn't even as nice as mine.

Then I hear a scratching noise followed by some whimpering, and I remember I'm supposed to be looking for my wedding gift.

Chapter Twenty-Five

I follow the sound to its source and discover a small caged enclosure on the other side of the tub, with newspapers on the floor and a dish of water, a dish of puppy chow, a blanket that's been chewed on and a chew toy that hasn't.

And a puppy. A sweet little dark-eared chunk who looks like a miniature version of Azi, only fuzzy. I scoop her up and she stops whimpering and buries her face against my chest, at which point I realize I'm still just wearing that torn piece of sheet and my tattered slip, not that it matters because nobody is around.

I carry the puppy back out to the bedroom, my heart swelling with appreciation at Ram's thoughtfulness, tempered with the desperate hope that he'll live long enough for me to thank him. For a while, the puppy and I just sit on the bed watching Ram breathe, and hoping he'll live. I'm glad for the soft little furball because she makes me feel slightly less alone in the cavernous fortress.

Then after a bit I realize I'm starving and the puppy and I head to the kitchen and check the fridge, which is stocked with steaks. Since I'm still a little rough on the fire breathing, especially in human form, I use the stove (which is this seriously massive twelve-burner thing with a griddle and grill plate and regular gas burners) and I grill a couple of nice porterhouses, slap them on a platter, and carry it back to the bedroom with the puppy at my heels.

"Hey Ram, you hungry? I grilled us some steaks," I

call out as I enter the room, because even if he's unconscious, it just seems rude to carry food in and eat it without offering him any.

But to my total surprise (seriously, I came very close to dropping the steaks) a weak voice answers.

"Starving. I feel like I've been gored by a bull."

I rush over to his side, not even really sure it was Ram who spoke, because I've never heard his voice sound so weak before, and because, you know, he's supposed to be unconscious.

His blue eyes are open, ringed with exhaustion that bends into a smile when he sees me.

I smile back dumbly for a few moments, because even though this doesn't mean for sure he'll make it through the night, it still seems like a good sign to me. "You know there's not a bull in the world strong enough to gore you," I remind him once I find my voice. "Those were Ion's horns, I think."

"That's right. I remember. I think he was really trying to kill me."

"He almost did." I don't mention that his efforts might still have their intended effect. "Do you think you can eat?"

"I'm starving. Thirsty, too."

So I get him some water, and when he manages to swallow that without too much trouble, I cut him slender strips of steak and feed him slowly, which he insists is torture, but I don't want to hurt him. That becomes a theme for the night.

Somewhere about halfway through the first steak, when Ram has a little bit of meat juice next to his mouth, and I realize I don't have a napkin to wipe it away, I remember we haven't kissed yet. So I set the steak aside and climb up onto the bed next to him, and kiss him, a sort of meaty, beautiful, delicious kiss so perfect I want to keep going, but I know Ram needs to breathe and recover and take things slowly.

When I pull away he starts to reach for me, but his arm is bound and I don't want him straining any stitches, so just to be on the safe side I kiss him again. And again.

The steak is cold by the time we get back to finishing it, but neither of us care.

*

Epilogue

Ram made it through the night. And he was okay, even if I gave him a hard time about acting like a sixty-seven-year-old. And my dad came back the next morning to check on us, which was extra special because he brought me my backpack. It was nice to have something to wear besides shredded sheets.

My knowledge of the Azeri language returned quickly, which was helpful because the villagers all wanted to meet me and talk to me and tell me how much I've revived their hope for the future, which is super awesome but also completely humbling.

Eudora hasn't bothered us, and neither has Ion. My dad's spies are keeping an eye on them for us, and report they're both hiding out in their respective castles in Siberia, keeping to themselves and not causing any real trouble, though they're likely plotting revenge, or something. If I had my guess I'd say Eudora is probably frantically trying to develop a serum to change her back into a dragon. My dad says now that Eudora's a human, she'll probably start aging like one, so she'll have to work fast on that serum if she's going to get it done in time to do her any good.

The puppy grew and soon looked just like Azi, and we started calling her Azi, mostly because she reminded us so much of her grandmother. By the time she was fully grown my first egg hatched, and she became little Ram's best friend and guard dog.

Ram was a little disappointed we didn't have a girl, girl dragons being most severely underrepresented in the world, but I assured him we'd balance the genders eventually, and sure enough, our next three (yes, three!) eggs hatched into girls.

Followed by another boy.

See, I'm taking seriously this thing about being keepers of the flame and protectors of our people, and I want to make sure we don't go extinct, not if I can help it.

I believe the world needs more dragons.

I know it's a big switch from what I've said before, but I've learned a lot of things about dragons. Maybe we are relics, and not as civilized as some folks. We're certainly scary, especially when we haven't had our coffee yet, or if we think something is threatening someone we love.

But we also keep our people safe (at least when we're not attracting danger by our mere existence) and watch over them and provide for them. Our mad dragon skills come in handy quite a bit, like when somebody needs to get somewhere fast, we can fly them on our backs. Or if there's demolition work to be done, our tails are good at that. Our vision is handy for seeing things far away. We're good at fishing, too — we can catch enough fish for the whole village in one night, if we find a good fishing spot. And then we can roast those fish in seconds with the flames from our mouths.

I'm all the time learning new things about myself, and discovering things I can do just because I'm a dragon. And you know what? I'm not just *okay* with who I am — fire-breath, scales and all.

I love being a dragon.

THE END

Dear Reader,

I hope you enjoyed *Dragon*. As Ram explained to Ilsa, the dragon world is comprised of dragons and the people who love and support them. Ram and Ilsa are supported, not just by the Jitrnickas and the villagers in Azerbaijan, but by readers.

By *you*.

You, Reader, make these stories possible. Without readers to enjoy the stories and share them with their friends, the dragons and all their adventures will fade from memory. Seriously. I'm not even exaggerating.

The good news is, being a part of the dragon world is a lot easier than fighting yagi. All you have to do is read the stories. If you want to go a step further and be my hero, you can review the books, and share the books with your friends, too.

Look for book two of the Dragon Eye series, *Hydra,* and for the other books in this series and my related series, The Lost Dragons. I hope you enjoy each and every one.

Thank you so much for reading *Dragon*!

Finley

CPSIA information can be obtained
at www.ICGtesting.com
Printed in the USA
LVOW10s0827280317
528733LV00003B/373/P